The Fortuneteller In 5B

Other Apple Paperbacks
you will enjoy:

Risk N' Roses
by Jan Slepian

Cousins
by Virginia Hamilton

Afternoon of the Elves
by Janet Taylor Lisle

Secrets in the Attic
by Carol Beach York

The Fortuneteller In 5B

Jane Breskin Zalben

AN
APPLE
PAPERBACK

SCHOLASTIC INC.
New York Toronto London Auckland Sydney

I wish to acknowledge my agent Marilyn E. Marlow for her support over the years, these recent ones especially; two fellow writers who were my initial readers: Patricia Baehr and Pam Conrad; Carey Ayres—a librarian, friend, and reader; Adaire Klein, Coordinator of Library and Archival Services at the Simon Wiesenthal Center in Los Angeles; my editor, Brenda Bowen—a gift from above at a time when I needed one; and Carol Roeder—not just a marketing director, but a friend.

ISBN 0-590-46041-2

12 11 10 9 8 7 6 5 4 3 2 1   3 4 5 6 7 8/9

Printed in the U.S.A.   28

First Scholastic printing, November 1993

To my mother—
who came over on the boat
and has survived many things.
With love.

CONTENTS

CHAPTER ONE

The Fortuneteller in 5B

I'll never forget the night she moved into apartment 5B, the empty studio above ours. Mine and Mom's. It will be a year ago this coming Friday. I remember it clearly because it was Dad's birthday, and he would have been forty-three. She arrived during a terrible thunderstorm, like in one of those horror movies. *Tree limbs are thrashing. A shadowy figure lurks on foggy street corners. The sound of horses' hooves on cobblestones is heard in the background.* I peeked through the glass-paned door to our brownstone. A woman with smeared bright red lips, holding a worn leather suitcase under one arm and a crystal ball under the other, stood on the stoop. "I'm the new tenant!" she shouted. As she was fumbling with the key, I buzzed her in. Her cape smelled of moth-

THE FORTUNETELLER IN 5B

balls. She hunched over and pushed a small printed card in my face: MADAME VAN DAM, SPIRITUAL ADVISER. "I charge ten dollars for reading palms. Tea leaves and tarot cards are extra. A séance— well, you're too young to want to contact any dead spirits." Her nose was about four inches from mine. A beauty mark was on the tip of it. Or was it a wart?

Okay, I said to myself, Alexandria Pilaf, this isn't a movie; get it together. Instincts told me to run, but this was *my* house, safe and sound, so how could I yell at myself as I often did at the TV screen, "Dummy, get out of there before it's too late!"

"Just a minute," Madame Van Dam ordered in a thick accent, and went to pay the cab driver. She returned with an animal carrying case. Something black and furry with long floppy ears peered through the mesh. I could barely see its chocolate brown eyes in the dark. "Her name's Tabitha. She's a lop rabbit. Black cats are *so* unoriginal," she said as she smoothed raindrops off her cape and leaned an umbrella next to the door. Then she waved her hand in the air and began to climb the staircase in the hallway. Her long chiffon scarf floated past her, trailing along the banister. I carried Tabitha's case upstairs. Her whiskers tickled my fingers through the mesh holes. Suddenly Madame Van Dam swirled around. A halo of dim light from the hallway circled her frizzy gray hair. "Have you ever had your fortune told?" I shook my head no. "For you, we can work out an arrangement." Why me? What did she have in mind? That I'd walk her rabbit? Or polish her crystal ball?

Madame Van Dam unlocked the door of apartment 5B and motioned for me to follow her. I gazed around while Madame Van Dam took the case from my grasp and let Tabitha out. She hopped between mountains of cardboard cartons and old dusty furniture. Her dangling ears streamed behind as she dashed around. The one large room was freshly painted scarlet red. Madame Van Dam took several votive candles from a box, scattering them at different ends of the room. As she lit each one, shadows flickered on the walls, dancing to Tabitha's hopping rhythm.

"Who thought I'd be moving at my age?" Madame Van Dam said, tossing aside an embroidered shawl as she sprawled across the couch. She patted the seat for me to sit next to her. I sat at the far end. The worn burgundy velvet felt soft against my skin. The couch looked older than she did.

"Where did you move from?" I asked, clearing my throat.

"Right outside of Manhattan."

"Brooklyn?" I asked.

"Queens." She sighed. "The landlord sold the

building. Everybody buys their apartments nowadays. I had trouble finding another place to rent. Especially one where I could make a living easily from street traffic besides my regular customers. Even this one," she pouted, "five floors up."

Sometimes I got winded hiking to our fourth-floor apartment below hers. And at my age. I felt sorry for Madame Van Dam.

"See this shawl?" Madame Van Dam smoothed her hand across the flowers and colored birds. I moved my leg aside as the fringes touched my thigh. The shawl seemed too delicate to sit on. "I made it." She smiled proudly. "I learned from my parents in the Old Country. Rumania. I sew. Hems. Drapes. Anything." She paused. Her eyes twinkled in the candlelight. "And then of course there's my natural gift. Making contact with the other side."

"The other side?"

"The hereafter. Ghosts," she said.

My legs stiffened. Was she putting me on? Or was she for real? "Well, I'd better be going." Maybe she was some kind of screwball?

Madame Van Dam got a far-off expression and then said, "Thank you," as she turned several latches so I could leave.

As I went downstairs to my apartment, the heavy odor of her perfume lingered and made me sneeze. I smiled at the thought of having my future revealed by this exotic person. Together we'd peer into her glass ball, and maybe I'd find out if Robby Berkert liked me, and if Dad was happy?

Then I thought that she probably couldn't read minds at all, and had about as much power as a sixty-watt bulb, because she was wrong about one thing: I wasn't too young to want to talk to a ghost and "make contact with the other side," as she put it. Then maybe I'd know where my father had been since he died almost six months before she arrived that night. Was he a twirling electrical force in the universe? Or was he like himself, in his khaki pants and faded plaid shirt, smiling at me when I made a goal during a soccer game or played a piece on the piano without any mistakes? I think I wanted to imagine him rolling around on soft clouds in the sunlight just like I did on the Castle Bounce this past spring. Our school had a fair to raise money. They set up an enormous inflated yellow-and-green raftlike rubber castle in the park, which me and a whole bunch of other kids jumped on barefoot. I felt free, like floating on a wave, suspended, waiting for the next one to come, the fear and the excitement of not knowing. It was just the kind of thing my father would have loved watching me on. There wasn't a summer that he didn't take me on some

THE FORTUNETELLER IN 5B

Ferris wheel or to a boardwalk with hot dogs, Italian ices, and pink cotton candy.

I asked my mother one night at dinner, "Do you think Madame Van Dam could help me speak to Dad?"

Mom's face paled. Slowly, she twisted some spaghetti around her fork and asked simply, "Why?"

"Why not?"

"Because." She paused. "Let things be, Alex." That's what she sometimes called me for short. My friends call me Allie. Last year at camp my counselor nicknamed me Sandy, and that stuck, but just for the two months.

Dad used to say, "How's my Big Al doing?" Mom said that sounded like I should belong to a club in Miami Beach and have a cigar and a diamond pinky ring and play gin rummy. So he stopped doing it, in public. When we were alone cuddling at night, he'd ask me that question, and I'd go on and on about my day until he'd have to shut me up. He'd kiss me on the nose near my freckles, trying to count how many I had until I drifted off to sleep.

Several weeks after Madame Van Dam arrived, a huge brown truck delivered a trunk for her. Its heavy lock rattled with each movement toward the brownstone as my best friend, Jenny Bolero, and I watched from my living-room window.

"Lady," the driver shouted, "what have you got in here, a body?"

Jenny shot me a quick glance.

"I'm not trudging up to the fifth floor for no one."

"Carry it to the basement and store it next to the washing machine," she said, slipping him some money.

"Laundry should definitely be the first item of business on our list of things to do," Jenny said with assurance.

As soon as we were sure they were gone, we went downstairs to the basement and loaded sheets and pillowcases into the machine. While I poured detergent on a ruffled sham, Jenny bent down on all fours examining the trunk. "You think there is a body inside?"

"Wouldn't it smell?" I teased.

"What if the remains decayed to just bones or dust? Mummies in museums don't have any odor. Are real people stuffed inside those bandages anyway?" Jenny asked.

We both shuddered at the thought.

Jenny lowered her voice. "Did you hear her accent? She could be an understudy for Count Dracula. What if it's dirt from her homeland?"

THE FORTUNETELLER IN 5B

"What, the borough of Queens?"

"No. *Not Queens*. You know," Jenny glanced over her shoulder, "Transylvania. Like in vampires. This could be the original soil from her coffin." And she made funny sucking noises.

"Oh, Jen, I heard her clumping around above me while I was eating breakfast. Wouldn't a real vampire be asleep during the daytime?"

"Maybe she's a witch, then."

"She's a fortuneteller. And a seamstress."

"That's what she says." Jenny continued to crawl on her hands and knees on the cement floor, checking every square inch of Madame Van Dam's trunk. Then she tapped the top.

"Come in," I said in a low, deep voice.

Jenny ignored me. "Look at all these dents. The brass is tarnished. These labels are foreign. Maybe there is something weird inside and we should call your mother?"

"And tell her what, that we were snooping around? Don't you think if Madame Van Dam had something to hide, she'd be more secretive?"

"Possibly," Jenny said, unconvinced, and she ran up the steps from the basement.

We slammed the door behind us.

The next day, the trunk was gone.

I telephoned Jenny immediately. "Maybe you were right."

"About what?"

"About something weird going on. It completely vanished. Disappeared!" I shouted into the receiver.

"What's gone?" She yawned.

"The trunk. I went downstairs to get a sock that was missing, and next to the washing machine was an empty space. What do you make of that?" I asked.

"Calm down, Alexandria Pilaf."

" 'Calm down,' she tells me. She's *my* neighbor, not yours. My time could be limited on this earth. One spell and *poof*, I could be a glass paperweight on my mother's mantelpiece for eternity."

"To think you might never date." Jenny sighed. "Not to mention, you could miss this season's soccer games."

"Jenny Bolero," I yelled into the phone, "I could miss soccer games for the next century!"

Suddenly, the phone went dead. Was this an omen?

CHAPTER TWO

Frogs, Bats' Brains, and Amulets

"What happened yesterday?" Jenny asked as she stood behind me on line in the school cafeteria. "I tried calling you after we were cut off." She balanced her tray next to mine. "Do you think it was *her*?"

"My mother said telephone wires can get messed up if they're wet, and it's been a damp April."

"This requires further investigation."

"Like what? We can't follow Madame Van Dam twenty-four hours a day." Jenny's eyes lit up at the suggestion. "No, Jen. We can't. Remember little things like school?"

"All I'm saying is that we take a simple trip to the library, go through the card catalogue, and look up anything that has to do with the super-

Frogs, Bats' Brains, and Amulets

natural." I rolled my eyes. "Be there at four," she ordered.

When I got home from school, my mother was sitting at the kitchen table with our neighbor from upstairs.

"Hi, sweetheart," Mom said. "Madame Van Dam made her own brew of herb tea. Would you like a sip? Dandelion and cherry leaves from Central Park."

Madame Van Dam looked straight at me as I poked the Baggie on the table, inhaling its contents. "And a few sprigs of rosemary from the pot on my windowsill over the kitchen sink," she added, tucking her caftan under her legs. Would that qualify for a traditional witch's robe? It wasn't a hooded cloak of some rough homespun cloth. It looked more like a cotton muumuu from Hawaii. The red and white flowers were a bit splashier than the usual basic black.

My mother sipped her tea. Returning the cup to its saucer, she smiled at me and said, "I got an assignment this morning to draw herbs for an article in *Horticulture Today*. I met Madame Van Dam as we both were taking out the garbage, and I was so thrilled I told her the news. And now she's made a gracious offer for me to use her plants as models." Dad always said that Ma was one of the best botanical illustrators around. She once painted

THE FORTUNETELLER IN 5B

an apple so real, I wanted to take a bite out of it.

I studied Madame Van Dam as her earrings jingled like wind chimes while she too sipped her tea. Her skin was dark and tight. Not wrinkled like an old person's. And her eyes were like black olives. I couldn't tell what was going on behind them. With some people, you could imagine what they were thinking from looking into their eyes, but not with her. Even though Madame Van Dam had lived here for almost a month, she kept mostly to herself. Maybe she was busy with moving to a new neighborhood? Unpacking. Whatever. But her being here in my kitchen seemed odd. Did she know Jenny and I had inspected her trunk? Did she see us in her crystal ball? Our every move? What if she wasn't simply some old woman in a fifth-floor walk-up who was trying to make a living telling fortunes and sewing people's hems? All sorts of people were starting to come and go to the top floor. And at strange hours, too. Like dinnertime. Who needs to know their future when they should be at home eating lamb chops? I thought of the story of Svengali. He had this mysterious power over young women, who would do anything for him. Did Madame Van Dam hypnotize her customers? Would she take over my mother's soul so that she wasn't really my mother anymore, but someone who just resembled her, like in the movie *Invasion of the Body Snatchers?* Maybe Jenny was right about her being a witch or a vampire. And I could become an orphan all because my own mother needed to illustrate potted parsley and thyme for the summer issue of some stupid gardening magazine, I thought as I grabbed a banana.

"I'm meeting Jenny at the library at four," I said.

"Just be home before it gets dark."

I glanced in the direction of Madame Van Dam to see if there was a glimmer of excitement at the mere mention of pending nightfall, checking Jenny's vampire theory, but her expression remained unchanged.

"Don't worry, Ma," I mumbled as I closed the door.

"You're ten minutes late," Jenny scolded when I found her in the 133.4 section of bookcases lined up in the children's room, pulling books off the shelf. "I started without you."

"I have a good excuse. *She* was in my house. In my kitchen. Sitting in the very seat where I eat cornflakes."

"You're lucky you're here, then," whispered Jenny as we heard a *shush* on the other side of the bookcase.

THE FORTUNETELLER IN 5B

"I left my own mother alone with that person, sipping some concoction. For all I know she's stretched out on the linoleum floor, poisoned."

Jenny balanced the pile of books in her lap and narrowed her eyes. She seemed to be more interested in the books about wizards, warlocks, chants, and flying ointments than in the fate of my mother.

"Get this," she said, thumbing through pages of love potions. "If you slip one of your hairs into Robby Berkert's bed, he'll fall in love with you." she giggled.

I punched her in the arm. "Be quiet!" I looked to see if anyone was around. "That couldn't happen in a zillion years, because the closest I've ever been to him is when he stepped on my foot on line as we waited for the pizza special in school." Then I remembered the time in assembly when his class sat near mine. I got to watch the back of his head for forty minutes, and the way his hair fell over the collar of his shirt. But I kept that to myself.

"You must add an egg and some rosemary to this hair," Jenny continued.

"Rosemary? Let me see that." I grabbed the book from her lap. "Madame Van Dam put rosemary in my mother's tea!"

"Does your mother want to be in love?"

"With whom?" I shoved the book aside. I thought of my father and how he liked to take long

Frogs, Bats' Brains, and Amulets

walks with Mom near the Boat House in the park, and how now she took them all alone, or with me. She is in love. Still. With my father.

We sat side by side and continued to search the shelves, mostly finding books on the history of witchcraft. One chapter was about amulets and talismans. There were pictures of lucky charms, coins, stones, jewels, a five-pointed star, and a rabbit's foot. I thought of Tabitha and her beautiful, oversized silver paws. Then I turned to a page and stopped.

"This looks almost exactly like Madame Van Dam's amethyst ring. The one she wears on her middle finger."

Jenny read the caption at the bottom of the page: *"Witches don't need to wear funny clothes. Your next-door neighbor could be one, and you might not know it!* What did I tell you!" Jenny looked triumphant. "She could put an evil eye on you while you're sleeping. You could wake up the next morning as a salamander in your science project. How do you know her rabbit is actually a rabbit, and not an heir to a throne? This could be serious. Here's a whole bunch of recipes to make a witch's power vanish." Jenny pointed to a list of ingredients. "Liver of frog, heart of toad, tongue of snake, brain of bat, with a couple of thorns thrown in."

"Thorns are easy," I chimed in, fueling Jenny's

doubts. "We could get them from the climbing rose-bush in front of the schoolyard. But the others—come on. What am I supposed to do, go to the butcher and ask, 'Excuse me, but are the frogs' livers fresh today?'"

"There must be some unusual butchers," Jenny insisted, smiling coyly. "My mother once had pheasant, quail, and frogs' legs at a dinner party. I guess we could come up with our own recipes, and pray they work."

"Jenny, why do I go along with you?"

"Because I'm your best friend."

We both laughed.

"Ask your mother if you can sleep over Friday night. We'll go through my kitchen cabinets and see if we can come up with potions." She looked at me innocently as we walked over to the checkout desk to take home some books. "You just never know when they'll be needed."

I pretended I had no idea what she was talking about, but we both knew who Jenny had in mind for those spells: Robby Berkert. Madame Van Dam.

CHAPTER THREE

Friday-Night Sleepover

The rest of the week went by pretty normally except for Jenny's hysterical call on Thursday evening. "I just found out that my parents got tickets to the ballet. They're having a late-night supper at some club afterward. They said they might be home by two in the morning and that I'd have to have a *baby-sitter*! Do you believe it? I'm twelve. I'd be fine all alone with you."

"Maybe that's what they're afraid of."

"Can we do the sleepover at your house?"

I put my hand over the mouthpiece. "Ma, can Jenny sleep over tomorrow night?" Mom nodded while she continued to paint some coriander or oregano. I could barely tell any of them apart. "She said yes."

THE FORTUNETELLER IN 5B

"Great!" Jenny exclaimed. "One problem solved."

"What's the other?"

"Getting rid of your mother so we can make the potions."

"See you tomorrow," I said, and hung up.

After dinner on Friday, Jenny's parents dropped her off on their way downtown to Lincoln Center.

As Jenny rushed into my room, chucking her overnight bag next to the dust ruffle, we heard a loud, steady thumping sound. "Was that my bag landing, or did it come from above the ceiling?" she asked.

We glanced up at the hanging lamp in the center of my bedroom ceiling and heard a distant noise. Jenny looked at me nervously. "Am I sleeping in a haunted house tonight? And my parents thought I'd be safe and sound *here*?" Then it happened again. "I'm zipping my sleeping bag over my head."

"You'll asphyxiate," I insisted, plopping down on my bed. Jenny sat next to me cross-legged, holding my pillow.

"Loss of consciousness is better than a slow and painful death at the mercy of some demon who needs to be exorcised from your plasterboard."

"Jenny," I shook my head, "you're so"—I tried to search for the right word—"you."

Friday-Night Sleepover

"Dramatic is the word. My mother says my name with the same look on her face. It's my roots," Jenny stated as she swung my long stuffed caterpillar around her shoulders, pretending it was a feather boa.

Her mother ran an agency, *Tangents,* that found offbeat people for television commercials and movies. Weirdos. Like this guy who could have doubled as a rodent and acted in an advertisement for pest control called Bug Off. Jenny contemplated using Bug Off on Madame Van Dam if she turned out to be a vampire or a witch, but I told Jenny that if she got caught, they would cut off her braided ponytail in reform school. So that settled that.

When the thumping ended, Jenny and I began to giggle, and we just couldn't stop. We rolled all over my bedspread, bumping into each other. Jenny landed on the floor, holding her stomach. I thought of how my mother told me that laughter is sometimes a release of anxiety, when that happened in the bathroom of the funeral parlor while I was washing the tears from my face before the service at Dad's funeral. My cousin Jeffrey had stuck his hand through a hole in the wall above the sink. When I saw fingers wiggling near the soap dispenser, I screamed. Then I couldn't stop laughing. The laughter hurt. I remembered thinking, This is awful. But

THE FORTUNETELLER IN 5B

I just couldn't help it. The principal at the high school where my father taught math must have thought I was this horrible obnoxious kid when he saw me leaving the ladies' room smiling.

Jenny tossed the pillow aside and grabbed my hand. "Don't ask questions, just follow me."

"Where are you taking me?" I asked as she pulled me into the hallway outside the apartment. I didn't want to make a fuss since my mother was in front of her drawing board. When she was working like that, it was almost as though she were sleeping because she got kind of out of it.

"What are we doing here?" I whispered.

"Stay close. Trust me," Jenny whispered back.

Jenny inched her way up to the top floor. We paused on the middle steps, spying between the spindles of the banister.

"Get back!' She waved her arm as we saw the bottom of a pair of red high heels disappearing into apartment 5B. I tugged at Jenny's sweatshirt. "Let go—you're going to make me fall."

"Maybe it will knock some sense into you. Why are we here?" I asked again, getting no answer from Jenny. She was too busy tiptoeing to the top landing. Foreign-sounding music was playing: the kind you hear in those movies with bands of gypsies circled in old covered painted wagons around campfires in the woods. Or a waiter is strolling in candlelit restaurants playing the violin. Sometimes Jenny sounded like that when she practiced her cello. My feet started perspiring on the scratchy carpeting that lined the hallway as I watched Jenny, also barefoot, with her ear to the door of apartment 5B. Oh God, I thought, if anyone comes out, we're sunk.

Loud laughter came from inside the apartment. Then suddenly the locks were being unlatched. Jenny and I froze. I yanked her hand and rushed to hide behind the heavy iron ladder going up to the roof. Jenny was about to sneeze, so I slapped the palm of my hand over her mouth as the large wooden door to 5B slowly opened. A mysterious woman with a wide-brimmed felt hat and dark netting covering her face kissed Madame Van Dam on one cheek, and then the other. It was the woman with the red shoes. This time I noticed a thin strap buckled around each ankle. They were dancing shoes. "*La revedere*, my silver jewel," she said between deep breaths in a husky voice. "See you when you're done with my costume."

"Don't worry; I won't make it too short. *Pa*." Madame Van Dam quickly closed the door, clicking each lock in turn.

Jenny and I slumped against the ladder. Each of us let out a deep sigh. Jenny wiped her mouth. "You nearly suffocated me."

THE FORTUNETELLER IN 5B

"Sorry." I listened to my heart return to its normal rhythm.

"What do you think she meant by 'my silver jewel'?" Jenny asked.

"I don't know," I said, swallowing some saliva.

"Did you hear her accent too?"

"Maybe she's a friend from her old neighborhood," I said.

"Transylvania or Queens?" Jenny asked.

"Queens, of course," I said impatiently.

"Well, I'm not waiting around to find out."

Jenny tore down the steps into my apartment. I followed her.

We slumped into kitchen chairs opposite each other. I heard the water trickling in the bathtub, which meant my mother was taking one of her lingering, hot baths and probably reading a thick novel while she was in the tub. She liked to do this after she worked all day.

My throat felt like sandpaper. I got ice cubes and glasses and poured us each a soda. Jenny finally broke the silence. "If there's one thing I'm certain of, it's this: we're going to need a very potent formula against that woman."

I let out a laugh.

"You wouldn't have found that so funny ten minutes ago," Jenny continued. "I felt you trembling."

"Trembling?" I said.

"Trembling," Jenny insisted.

She got up on the stepladder and began opening the doors to the kitchen cabinets.

"What are you looking for now?" I asked.

"Where does your mother keep all her stuff other than dishes?"

"Over there." I pointed to a narrow oak cabinet on the wall, which held cereals, turquoise-colored Ball jars filled with beans, grains and rice, spices and herb teas.

"Cayenne pepper is good and hot. My dad uses it in his chili."

"My mother told me that if you sprinkle it on tulips, it keeps the squirrels from eating the flowers," I said.

"They don't like spicy food?" Jenny laughed at her own joke as she reached for a jar of peanut butter, handing it to me.

"What concoction are you dreaming up?" I asked as she added honey and maple syrup to my armload of food.

"Hides the taste of bitter ingredients," she murmured. "A potion for your neighbor, and one for you."

"For me?" I glared at Jenny while she came down from the stepladder. "What have you got against me?"

THE FORTUNETELLER IN 5B

"Silly," she said as she plucked a reddish brown hair from my head. "Nothing."

"Ouch!" I cried. "Have you gone crazy?"

"No, but Robby Berkert will if this potion works. He'll be your love slave forever."

"*Jen-ny!*" I shouted at the very idea of her even saying his name out loud.

"I'm your best friend. Come on. I know."

"Okay," I admitted, "but then he won't like me of his own free will."

"Who cares? Worry about that when he asks you to the movies."

"No one's asking me anywhere. I'm too young to go on a date."

"I didn't mean a *date* date. I meant when you go in a group and maybe he sits next to you and shares his popcorn and spearmint leaves. Or asks you to dance at Denise Miller's party at the end of the year."

"Sixth graders don't go to seventh graders' parties."

"They do if a potion works."

"Oh." I dreamed of Robby's blond hair and blue eyes and the way he smiled when he had sung in the school chorus at the spring concert. If any potion could make him smile at me like that, then it might be worth every hair on my head. Well, just a few strands.

Friday-Night Sleepover

"We need something to put this stuff in when we're done mixing."

I knocked on the bathroom door. "Ma, can I come in?"

"Uh-huh," she said in this dreamy tone. A misty haze coated the mirror on the wall. I looked for a couple of empty pill containers in the medicine cabinet and found two small ones with Dad's name on the prescription label. I sighed as I took them off the shelf.

When I came out of the bathroom, Jenny was quickly stirring some ingredients in the stainless-steel bowl my mother ordinarily used for mixing yeast breads. "Hurry up," I said, "my mother's at the point in her bath where she could play a prune in one of your mother's commercials."

Jenny grabbed a mixing spoon and stuffed a thick, yucky brown glob into one of the pill containers. I snipped a strip of white masking tape from the roll on my mother's drafting table and placed a piece over the label that read, IAN PILAF: TAKE ONE EVERY FOUR HOURS FOR PAIN. Jenny wrote in black Pointel: R. B.'S LOVE POTION. On the second pill bottle she drew a skull and crossbones and lettered: COUNTERPOTION. She mumbled an incantation:

"Toil, toil, aluminum foil,
Make the vampire above us boil."

THE FORTUNETELLER IN 5B

She swirled her hands in the air high above the other plastic cylinder, which still had in tiny print at the bottom: SIDE EFFECTS: NAUSEA. Then I thought of Dad getting thinner and thinner, his skin yellowing, and not being able to eat. I tried to erase that image from my mind and focus on Jenny as she waved her arms and closed her eyes. Her fingers glided in the air like a belly dancer, twisting and turning. Then she opened her eyes and dabbed a tiny bit of mush on the center of my forehead. It smelled like yesterday's breakfast. As the oatmeal dripped on my eyebrows, Jenny recited:

"Honey dripping on a vine,
The Berkert boy will soon be thine."

The potion began to dry like plaster on my skin, and I remembered my father filling rubber molds for me in our old basement for a set of farm animals that he, Mom, and I painted together when they were dry. "My mother is going to come out any second," I said as I heard the water begin to drain.

Jenny's eyes fluttered.

"Mustard seeds upon thy head . . ."

Friday-Night Sleepover

Oh, please make her hurry, I thought. And don't make her rhyme it with bed.

"These two souls, I thee wed."

The bathroom door was flung open. A gush of warm air swept into the kitchen. The curtains over the sink became limp.

"No, Jenny," I muttered, "it's not a supernatural force, only moisture."

"What's going on here?" my mother asked as she made her way past the mess to the living-room couch, which doubled as her foldout bed.

"Baking," I said.

"For the school bake sale," Jenny added. "We're raising funds for a class trip."

"To where?" asked my mother. "With this much batter, to Alaska?"

"To some preserve in the Adirondacks. We're doing a nature study." I knew that would get my mother. Anything that had to do with molds and fungi.

"Just make sure the kitchen is the way you found it."

"We will," Jenny said politely.

"And wash your face, Alex. You've got batter all over your forehead."

THE FORTUNETELLER IN 5B

Jenny and I gave each other a look, and then glanced away in separate directions so we wouldn't crack up. As soon as the bathroom cooled off, my mother went in and switched on the blow-dryer, closing the door behind her.

I let out a sigh of relief. "That was a close call."

"You're telling me," Jenny said as she began to rinse the dishes and hand them to me. I stacked them in the dishwasher. "Won't your mother become suspicious when she doesn't smell anything baking?"

"I didn't even think of that," I said.

"We'll say they're special icebox cookies."

"Quick thinking, Jen." I patted her on the back.

Before we went to sleep, Jenny leaned toward my pillow. "I had fun tonight." And she poked my arm gently.

"So did I."

"Remember the water table at nursery school when we spilled water from one plastic tub to another?"

"Sure." I smiled, remembering coming home with soaked cuffs on my polo shirts on those mornings.

"You think all this stuff about potions and Madame Van Dam is silly, don't you, Allie?"

I shrugged. "Who knows anything, Jen? What's real, what isn't?"

Friday-Night Sleepover

There was a big part of me that wanted to believe in magic. It was like being five again, when I put petals from my father's red rosebush in the blender and sold the mush on our street corner for 25 cents a tiny bottle. I told everybody that it was perfume, and started thinking it was after a while. As I turned away from the glow of the streetlight through the window and tried to go to sleep, I realized I was hoping our magic worked—mine and Jenny's—even if it was made up. That it wasn't like a card trick, with a logical answer. It was sort of the same feeling I had when I knew my father was going to die of cancer. I prayed to God that he wouldn't, and kept pretending that it would never happen— that some unreal force out there would solve every- thing—half of me believing, half of me not. I wanted to believe that Madame Van Dam was some mystical being, that maybe she knew a truth I didn't.

I thought of when Dad read me *Peter Pan*, and the part when Peter begs us all to clap louder and louder if we believe in fairies so Tinkerbell won't die. It says in the book: "Many clapped. Some didn't."

CHAPTER FOUR

The Street Fair

My mother peeked from beneath her patchwork quilt while Jenny and I made pancakes. The early morning sun sparkled on the spider plant hanging near her drafting table and the striped rag rug on the floor. I filled her mug—which had a large black *L* for Lorna on the front—with hot coffee and put it at her place setting.

"Pour vous," I said, moving out a carved chair she and Dad had found at a flea market in Soho for his birthday. A red-and-white checkered dish towel was draped over my arm.

"Fancy-pancy." My mother looked surprised. Jenny smiled as she poured the orange juice. "Did you sleep well?" Mom asked her.

"Fine, Mrs. Pilaf."

The Street Fair

"No bats? No rattling chains at midnight?" I muttered.

Jenny looked as if she wanted to pour the juice on my head.

"Thanks for having me over. I'm sorry about the mess last night."

We couldn't help noticing the near-empty bottle of maple syrup, most of which had been used for the counterpotion.

"Where are those cookies, or whatever you baked, anyway?" Mom gazed at the bare countertop. "Maybe you could sell some for the Community Association's street fair today. Last night you seemed to be mixing up enough for your school bake sale and our entire neighborhood."

On the refrigerator was a flyer dangling beneath a row of magnets in the shapes of fruits and vegetables.

Block Party May 1. Rain date, May 8.
Plant a Tree on West 76th Street.
Your Neighborhood Counts!
Sponsored by Citizens for a More Beautiful
Environment

"We can't," I said nervously.

"We just couldn't," chimed in Jenny.

"Why not?" Mom looked at me questioningly.

THE FORTUNETELLER IN 5B

"The money we make from the school bake sale will go to planting a pine forest and nourishing some poor little starving saplings in upstate New York."

Jenny pretended to play the violin behind my mother.

Mom shook her head as she sipped the last drops of coffee. "How about nurturing some trees in your own backyard?"

I thought of the potions at the bottom of Jenny's overnight bag, instead of our phantom cookies, and how I lied. "Gotta go."

Jenny gulped down her juice. "Me too."

"Where's the fire?" Mom asked.

"The soccer game's in half an hour. Want to come?" I asked.

"Oh, sweetie, I wish I could, but I've got this detailed sketch due by Monday. Some other artist screwed up and drew the *Galanthus nivalis* as a June perennial, when obviously it's an early March flower."

Jenny looked at her blankly.

"Common snowdrop," I said, having been raised on the terminology of the plant kingdom.

My mother and I would dissect flowers and examine them under the microscope. She made glass slides of leaves and bugs, focusing the lens for me as I gazed into her magnified world. Sometimes she'd give me some of her good drawing paper and I'd sketch a wing or the veins of a leaf, trying to make them look alive, just like my mother did.

"See you later," I said with one foot out the door.

"Thanks again, Mrs. Pilaf." Jenny rushed after me.

The field was crowded when we got there. The Yellow team was already practicing, passing the ball. Cynthia Wellsley gloated as she gave it a good kick right into the net. Everyone shouted, wishing it were the real game and she had made a goal. Jenny ran toward her father, giving him a big hug and her overnight bag to hold. He handed her our team shirt, which she'd forgotten to pack. THE GREEN MACHINE was printed on it. When he put his arm around Jenny's shoulders, tossing her a soccer ball, I got this pang inside. Dad would have been waiting on the sideline with a thermos of iced lemonade or a plastic water bottle for me to squirt in my mouth at halftime. He would have smiled proudly if I'd scored a goal for my team. My eyes became blurry, wanting him here with me, something that could never be. I took a deep breath and swallowed hard as I walked onto the field, taking my position.

As usual, fifteen minutes into the second half

THE FORTUNETELLER IN 5B

of the game, Cynthia's mother had a disagreement with the referee. Voices got louder and louder as parents from both sides became involved. The coaches tried to remind the adults that we were here to have fun. They were setting a bad example of team spirit. Jenny and I kept making weird faces at each other, imitating the grown-ups, as we stood on the field kicking tufts of grass and waiting for them to finish yelling. Mrs. Wellsley got her way. We lost by one point. The score was the Yellow Barracudas, 5, the Green Machine, 4.

"It's just a game," Jenny's father said, stroking her back.

"I know." She shrugged, kicking her ball as she walked.

"Come on," he said to both of us.

We followed him as he headed for a silver cart with a bright pink umbrella. HOMEMADE ITALIAN ICES was written across the side. "One lemon, please," Jenny ordered. You could see real bits of shredded pulp as she squeezed the white paper cup, licking the mound of frosted ice.

"Chocolate chip," I said, eying the bittersweet drops swirled in creamy vanilla.

Jenny's father paid the man when I offered some money. "This one's on me."

"Thank you, Mr. Bolero."

"Anytime," he said. "It's not every day I get

to treat two such pretty girls." And he winked at both of us.

"Oh, Dad," Jenny groaned.

We walked from the park toward Columbus Avenue, which was a block from my house. My street was roped off so that cars couldn't drive through. A large banner with the slogan OUR FUTURE GROWS was strung across the street. A sea of green balloons dotted the sidewalk. Each one had a picture of a small tree. Long wooden tables were lined up and down the block.

"Can we go?" Jenny begged her father.

"Sorry, hon—we plan to visit your grandmother."

Jenny looked disappointed. "I'll call you," she said to me. "Have fun."

"Bye." I waved, knowing it wouldn't be the same without her.

As Jenny and her father left, I strolled past stands of secondhand books, earrings for pierced ears, and quilted pot holders. Behind a folding table—like the kind I had at my birthday parties when I was little—a man was stuffing salad and falafel balls into pita bread.

"I'll have a half," I said. When he handed me the pita, some tahini dripped on my shirt. I dabbed the sesame sauce with a napkin. "And a small Coke, please."

THE FORTUNETELLER IN 5B

I searched for a place to sit and found the bottom steps of the brownstone where I lived vacant. As I munched on my sandwich and stared at a fire hydrant a neighbor had painted red, white, and blue, a jug band played across the street. Someone was blowing into a large glass jug while another person whistled into a microphone. There was a tin washtub with a long neck, reminding me of Jenny's cello. A young guy plucked the strings. Another boy about my age was tapping out the rhythm with a pair of spoons. The man next to him, wearing a denim cowboy shirt and a red paisley handkerchief knotted around his neck, picked at a fiddle, while another man fingered a reed instrument that looked like the recorders Mrs. Rooney gave to everyone in music class at school. A woman with blond hair sang. The crowd clapped while a baby who looked as if she had just learned to stand bobbed up and down. My heart suddenly began to pound. Robby Berkert was on the other side of the street with two younger boys in the sixth grade. I wiped my lips with the napkin and swushed Coke around my mouth in case there were any tiny bits of salad stuck between my teeth. More people crowded in front of me listening to the music as I tried to sneak a glimpse of Robby. The band stopped. I crumpled the paper wrapper filled with crumbs of falafel balls. Then I noticed six sneakers lined up on the sidewalk

The Street Fair

in front of me. Squinting in the sun's glare, I faintly made out the outline of Robby's denim jacket.

"Hi," I said, trying to keep cool inside. My cheeks felt flushed.

"Hi," he answered, stuffing his hands in his pockets. "You still have your soccer shirt on. Who won?"

I glanced at my green shirt. A small but obvious dried stain from the tahini was on my chest. I immediately folded my arms in front of me. "They did," I mumbled.

"What was the score?"

My mind went blank. This was the first time I had ever talked to someone I liked. Not anyone. A seventh-grade boy. Not any boy. Robby Berkert. Did it show? Did he notice? Worse, did his friends notice, and would they tease him and me afterward? And the whole school would know.

"Five to four," his friend interrupted, rescuing me without realizing it. "My cousin's on the Yellow team. They slaughter the Green every week."

"Tough luck." Robby shrugged. Freckles sprinkled his nose like mine. He had this cute way of smiling that made me feel all warm and nervous at the same time. "See you around." He turned to go.

"See you around," I said, not sure of what else I should say.

Robby Berkert had spoken to me. He actually

noticed me. Why? Thirteen-year-old boys don't really care about almost-twelve-year-old girls, do they? They like baseball cards, comics, Nintendo, and anything that has remotely to do with science fiction. Was he just being friendly? Why now? After a whole year of school. Did the love potion actually work? Wait until I tell Jenny, I thought. She'll faint.

I threw my Coke cup and wrapper into a garbage can beside Amsterdam Antiques. Mrs. Rose Pearlstein, our downstairs neighbor and mother of our landlords, the Blechmans, was sorting through china plates and pale rose-colored glass teacups stacked on a lace tablecloth spread across the stand she was running.

"Darling," she said, recognizing me immediately, "what can I do for you? Do you believe I'm working on a day like this with such a mob? I guess better a mob than empty. It's been nonstop traffic. A lot of lookers, not a lot of takers."

I smiled politely as I picked up an old hairbrush with thick yellow bristles and ornate silver carving of flowers and leaves on the back. "Pretty," I said, turning it around.

"There's a comb and mirror to match." Then Mrs. Pearlstein touched my arm and lowered her voice as though someone were listening. "Between you and me, who wants a brush where you don't know whose head it's been in. And old hair to boot.

The Street Fair

I have a rule: You lend personal toiletries to no one. Only family. Immediate family. You know what I mean?"

I nodded, thinking of the time the school nurse sent notes home with all of us when Heather Goldman got cooties. I remember Andrew Blechman told me his grandmother said, "A Jewish girl with head lice?" The nurse told us it had nothing to do with cleanliness, but the Blechmans fumigated the entire brownstone, and my mother washed nearly everything that wasn't nailed to the ground. Since then, I've shampooed my hair every night. I began to scratch my head just thinking about it.

"Do you have anything for Mother's Day? It's in a week," I said.

"Come to this end of the table." Mrs. Pearlstein beckoned with her finger. She showed me a tiny glass bottle. Painted on the front was a bough with white blossoms. Oriental letters ran down the side. An ivory stopper with a jade green glass top corked the bottle.

"What is this?" I was afraid even to hold it.

"A Chinese snuff bottle. Snuff. Makes you sneeze. Like pepper. Clears the sinuses on a day like today."

"Look at the delicate glass," I said in awe.

Mrs. Pearlstein raised her voice. "That's what makes this so special. The detail. We have some

THE FORTUNETELLER IN 5B

porcelain and cameo ones inside the glass cabinet over there. Very old."

"How much is it?" I asked. Mrs. Pearlstein told me.

"So, is it a sale?"

I paused, knowing my mother would love to stare at the snuff bottle, which she'd probably put on the windowsill in front of her drafting table. She'd especially like the way the tiny blossoms were painted.

"Can I give you half now and half maybe next week?" I asked.

"Why not? We're neighbors. I trust you. I know where to find you if you don't make good on the deal," she teased. As she carefully placed the bottle between two wads of cotton inside a small cardboard box, I noticed a tent set up next to us. There was a large hand-lettered sign: A FORTUNE A MINUTE. SEE INTO YOUR FUTURE. A crystal ball was drawn under the word *future*. Mrs. Pearlstein saw me looking as she Scotch-taped the lid. "What a *meshugana* that one is. A real nut. At least she pays her rent on time. And in cash, no less. She's from Rumania. If you ask me," she put her hand on my arm and lowered her voice, "a Gypsy. My parents told me they were always wandering all over Eastern Europe. No roots. Always kept to themselves in their tribes. Very different from us."

The Street Fair

What did she mean by that? *Us?* I wasn't like Mrs. Pearlstein.

Madame Van Dam a Gypsy! The word alone sent tingles down my spine. There was something so exciting about the idea of a Gypsy living right above me and Mom.

"But there's one thing that woman and I have in common."

If Jenny were here, she'd say, "Mrs. Pearlstein's a vampire too?"

"Hitler, that Nazi, he had us both at the top of his list. The Jews and the Gypsies. He wanted to get rid of all of us first."

Mrs. Pearlstein's face was tight now. Different from when she was showing me all those pretty antiques. I felt as if Mrs. Pearlstein had thrown cold water in my face. Shocked. I'm not sure why, because I knew from Sunday school about World War II, and how the Nazis killed six million Jews in concentration camps. We were told that six million other people were also murdered. I never knew about the Gypsies. Then for some stupid reason I thought of Cynthia Wellsley and her mother, and how there were always going to be people who tried to act like they were better than everyone else because deep down inside they knew they weren't. I also thought of Mrs. Pearlstein telling me how she trusted me to pay her back because we were neighbors. How come she didn't seem to trust Madame Van Dam? Weren't they neighbors too? Was it just because Madame Van Dam was different? Was that fair?

Mrs. Pearlstein tucked the box in my hand. Then she began to help a young man interested in sheet music from the early twenties. I put Mom's gift in my pocket where I knew it would be safe and stared at the canvas flap of the fortunetelling tent. Was a customer inside? I felt the way I had last Halloween when Jenny and I went trick-or-treating in her apartment building, and we were too scared to go to old man Brady in 12E because everyone said he gave out poison apples and Snickers with razor blades inside. A voice came from within the tent. "Enter."

Should I run away the way Jenny and I had that night, when Mr. Brady opened the door and said, "Girlie, want some candy corn?"

"Enter," Madame Van Dam's deep voice repeated. Slowly, I lifted the flap to the tent. "Come in," she said, putting down a newspaper in some foreign language.

There was a faint sweet smell. Like wild blackberries. The air was still. Almost humid. My hair began to frizz. I yanked at the top of my T-shirt, avoiding Madame Van Dam's deep-set eyes. When

The Street Fair

my eyes finally rested on her face, my mouth suddenly felt dry. "Hello," I managed to say.

"Sit down." She pulled out a folding wooden chair. Tabitha was underneath, munching on broccoli. I hesitated. "Closer," she said.

She wore a scarf on her head, large gold hoop earrings, a gold-coin necklace, a peasant blouse, and a skirt with ruffles at the hem. I stared at the flowers on her shirt. Two tiny tassels hung from the open neckline. She smoothed her hands around the crystal ball. On a finger was the amethyst ring I had told Jenny about. When she closed her eyes in deep concentration, I looked around the small tent. Copper ornaments, good-luck amulets, and colorful shawls decorated the sides. A picture of the Madonna was hanging on the wall, like in Jenny's church. My heart gave a sudden thump when Madame Van Dam stopped massaging the glass ball and quickly opened her eyes.

"I see a boy. A young boy. You like him. He likes you, too."

"He does?"

"Someone you know is gone. I'm not sure where. Through a dark tunnel. A bright light at the end. You want the person back. Give me your palm," she ordered.

I held out my hand, palm up, noticing beads

THE FORTUNETELLER IN 5B

of sweat in the middle, just like I used to get before a piano recital. No one had to be psychic to figure out that I was scared stiff. Where was Jenny when I needed her? Shopping at some mall with her grandmother? I cleared my throat. When she touched my palm, I got chills down my spine and goose bumps on my arms.

"You have a long life line. Many beautiful children. Many healthy grandchildren."

"How many children?" I asked in a tiny voice.

"Three, maybe four. And ten grandchildren."

"Gosh."

Would it be with Robby, ha ha? Her eyebrows drew together. The wrinkles in her forehead tightened, forming sharper creases in her dark skin. She pulled my hand closer, curving her fingernail over one of the lines in my palm. Was that my life line? And she'd tell me how long I had to live? "Is my minute up yet?" I asked, starting to feel uneasy and drawing away.

"You've had pain in your young life, like I did at your age." I felt myself tightening inside. I pulled back my palm. She tried to relax my fingers, gently smoothing hers over mine. In a slow, paced voice, the rhythm of it soaking me into her spell, I listened even though I could barely hear what she was saying. My head swirled as she continued. "Because you've lived through what most adults experience later on in life, you have gotten strength from this pain. And after pain, joy can come. With time." Was she talking about herself or me?

Madame Van Dam smiled. No gold tooth like a Gypsy. No fangs like a vampire. But not an ordinary person. That was for sure. How did she know *anything* about me? Had my mother told her Dad had died? Or had her crystal ball? I placed a dollar on the card table and said, "Thank you."

The table wobbled. She handed the money back to me. "Next time when I read your cards you can pay me."

Next time? There was no way Jenny was getting out of that. I didn't care who she had to visit. No way in the world.

CHAPTER FIVE

A Special Time

A note had been left on my mother's drawing table: *Finished the sketch earlier than expected. Going to browse at the fair and get a pizza. Don't eat. Be back soon. Love and XXX, Mom.*

Tired, I rested on the couch and read a book for a while, and then I dialed Jenny's number. On the sixth ring she answered. Sometimes she didn't hear it ringing while she was practicing her cello.

"Good, you're home," I said. "You won't believe what happened. Madame Van Dam read in a crystal ball that a boy likes me. She also read my palm and told me I'm going to have three or four children and ten grandchildren."

"Someone better if you're going to have that many children."

A Special Time

"Jenny," I grumbled into the mouthpiece, "I saved the best for last. Robby Berkert spoke to me."

There was silence at the other end of the line. Then a loud squeal. "He did? What did he say?"

" 'Who won the soccer game?' "

"That's what he asked you?"

"That, and the score."

"At least he spoke to you. See, the potion worked."

But I could hear disappointment in her voice. Maybe she had expected Robby to confess some inner passion after all our efforts the night before? Jenny was more experienced than me. She had once danced at her uncle's wedding with a boy two years older. And a month ago, she had spoken to Jason Rosenthal on the phone for a whole ten minutes. He called while we were doing our homework about an earth science project they were doing together. I remember her cheeks being flushed when she got off.

"Jenny, it was so weird with Madame Van Dam. It was like she knew about my father and Robby. You think she saw me talking to Robby?"

"Was the tent one of those see-through fabrics like the magicians use for their tricks?"

"It was a heavy canvas like we slept in at Brownie camp."

"Then she's psychic."

THE FORTUNETELLER IN 5B

"Do you really think so?" I asked, thinking that if she was, maybe I could talk to my father through her. And how good it would feel to ask him how he was doing. I hoped he didn't have any more pain.

"Allie, you were very brave to go into her tent alone."

"Thanks, but the truth is I felt safer knowing Mrs. Pearlstein was right outside. Oh yes, Madame Van Dam said that she would read her cards for me. And I don't care who needs you, Jen; this time you're coming."

"Do you think she would read mine too?"

"I guess we could ask," I said.

"This is even better than the time one of my mother's clients organized a séance. Get this—nobody had anyone they wanted to speak to on the other side. Could you imagine still being pissed off at relatives even after they're dead?"

And I thought, Yes. For leaving.

When I had hung up the phone, I got a queasy feeling inside, like I had spent the day on the Staten Island Ferry. Was it the falafel? Mom always said not to eat food that was sold on the street. My stomach felt crampy, so I went into the bathroom and started getting undressed to take a bath. I got a whiff of my soccer shirt as I threw it into the hamper under the sink. I hoped Robby Berkert didn't think I smelled like a mule. As I was taking off my underpants, I saw a dark brown stain, and I got kind of scared. I thought of Jenny's dog, Madge, who had to be dewormed last summer. Did I have worms? How could such a thing happen? No, it was a little clot of dried blood. When and where did I get a cut? As I bent down searching for the Woolite Mom used on her bras so I could rinse my panties in the sink, I noticed behind the rolls of toilet paper a box of sanitary napkins.

Mrs. Jackson, the school nurse, had given out some pamphlets a few weeks ago called "Your Teenage Menstrual Cycle." We were all so embarrassed, we read them quickly. No one actually said it out loud, but I could sense that we all felt the same thing: Did anyone really get her period before the end of sixth grade? There were rumors that Cynthia Wellsley had gotten hers. But she lied about everything.

I decided it was time for a closer look at the facts. I wrapped a large Snoopy beach towel around me and ran into my room, taking out the pamphlet hidden between my nightgowns and pajamas. Then I ran back and sat on the edge of the tub, because I was afraid of getting the toilet seat cover or bath mat stained, and examined the diagrams of the reproductive cycle to find out what was in store for me about every twenty-eight days from now on. The booklet even answered dumb questions about

THE FORTUNETELLER IN 5B

pimples, washing your hair during your cycle, dancing, horseback riding, and playing sports. But I guessed I shouldn't talk. I had thought I had worms.

"Alex, are you home?" I jumped when I heard my mother's voice.

"In here, Ma," I said, quickly locking the bathroom door.

She knocked and twisted the knob. "Hon, are you okay?"

"Uh-huh."

"Could you open up? I've got a headache and need to take something."

I threw the booklet in the cabinet under the sink and unlocked the door. Mom looked at me, one of her careful, examining looks, and pulled back my bangs. She pressed her lips against my forehead, as she had been doing since I was little, to see if I had fever. They felt soft and comforting against my skin.

"You seem warm to me. Are you sick?" Mom looked concerned.

"Just perspiring from running around at the fair today."

"Did you have a nice time?" she asked.

"Uh-huh."

"Maybe I should take your temperature just in case?"

"Ma, I'm okay."

A Special Time

"First let me get some Tylenol for me."

She went for the pills and the thermometer, and bent down to get a washcloth next to the hamper. She stopped, noticing the pamphlet that had fallen out of place.

"Sweetheart, what's up?" Mom had radar. Her little antennas picked up anything out of the ordinary in my behavior, like the time I was angry at her and fibbed about watering down her Chanel No. 5. Of course, she didn't have to be a genius to know that the golden brown perfume had become a pale yellow liquid. But she knew what I had done.

I glared down at the thick beige bath mat, twitching my toes through its shaggy threads. Mom put her arms around me and hugged me so tight that we both nearly toppled over into the bathtub. We started laughing. Her big brown eyes got all blurry. "Ma, are you okay?" She nodded. "Ma. I got my . . ." I had trouble getting the word out. She smoothed my back with her hand, and I swayed gently like a boat rocking in its slip.

"I know," she whispered. Her cheek touched my bangs as she held me, and I felt warm and protected. "Congratulations."

"You're sure you're okay?" I looked up at her.

"Are *you* okay?" Mom asked as she sat down on the toilet seat lid and blew her nose into a tissue. "Is there anything you need to know?"

THE FORTUNETELLER IN 5B

"Well," I paused, "how old were you when you got yours?"

"Hmm." She sighed. "About your age. I wasn't twelve yet. I remember that because it was the beginning of the sixth grade. I was seeing my first opera, 'Aida,' at the Metropolitan Opera House. My aunt Phyllis took my cousin Rachel and me. There were live elephants on the stage, and it was wonderful. I remember thinking, How did they get them inside the theater? At intermission I started feeling not myself. And that night, while my cousin and I were getting ready for bed, I went to the bathroom and realized I had gotten my period."

"What happened then?"

"My aunt helped me, showing me how to put the sanitary pad in the belt. Did they have tampons then?" Mom wondered out loud. "And then I called Grandma and Grandpa."

"What did they say?"

"Come home. But I slept over."

"Did it change you a lot?"

Mom laughed. "Inside or out?"

"Both," I said.

"I spent more time in the bathtub singing rock-and-roll songs behind the shower curtain and pining away for all the boys who didn't notice me. I also grew from an A cup to a B that year."

A Special Time

I thought of the three training bras in my drawer with the pretty bows and silk rosebuds in the center, and apricot lace trim, and how I didn't want to have to give them up.

"So it took a year," I repeated.

Good. My body wouldn't change overnight. I needed time getting used to it. I hoped that when it did change, and if Robby Berkert ever liked me, it would be because of me, and not what might happen to my body.

"Thanks, Ma."

"For what, you silly sweetie?" She hugged me again. "Why don't you relax in a nice warm bubble bath. I'll reheat the pizza, which is probably cold by now." And she closed the bathroom door.

I put a drop of Mom's peach bath oil into the water, looking at myself as I sank down. Blowing bubbles in the tub, playing with my toy boats and plastic people seemed so far away it made me sad. As the water pounded from the faucet, the steam almost hypnotized me, making my mind drift away. I thought, What would Dad have said about today? Would he have bought me a dozen red roses? And joked, "Now you're really my Big Al." Would Mom miss not being able to turn to him later tonight when she put her head down on her pillow and say, "Our little girl is growing up."

THE FORTUNETELLER IN 5B

When I came out of the bathroom and sat down at the kitchen table, I found a red Chinese cloisonné pin on my napkin. "What's this?"

Mom leaned over and pinned it on my terry-cloth robe. "Your father gave this to me when we were dating. I think he would have wanted you to have it now." She shifted back in her seat. "I'm sure he would have." There was a loud thump above our heads from Madame Van Dam's apartment. "You see, it's a sign." We both giggled.

After we ate our pizza, Mom pulled the couch out into a bed, and we watched a horror movie on TV. We ducked under the covers every time the swamp monster came on the screen. When it was over, I asked, "Ma, can I sleep here tonight? With you?" She wiggled her toes next to mine. Her nightgown felt like ribbons of soft gauze against my legs. As she wrapped her arm over my shoulder, the curve of my body fitting into hers, I whispered longingly, "I miss Dad."

"So do I." I could feel the warmth of her breath on the back of my neck.

"Did you ever tell Madame Van Dam about him?"

"Tell her what?"

"That he's dead."

"I think she knows. We were both in the front vestibule, and I commented how the mail keeps coming for him. I wondered if it would ever stop."

I turned and put my arm around her. "His L. L. Bean catalogues still come."

"So do all those tons of seed and bulb ones."

"Oh, Ma, you like those."

"Dad and I both did. He always liked the vegetable seeds. Practical. A math teacher. I always ordered tulips and wildflowers. An artist." She took a deep breath. "It's as though he weren't dead. Sometimes I pretend he went on a long business trip, and that he'll be coming back any day now. It doesn't seem real. It's hard having to learn to live with the fact that he's not here anymore."

Mom kept the flannel shirt from the last winter catalogue Dad ordered from, and I remember walking in on her in the bedroom closet and catching her sniffing the armpits. Sounds crazy, but I guess maybe the smell of Dad's sweat was still there. I wondered if she ever washed it. I know she hung it back in the closet and never gave that one away.

I looked over at the red pin on my bathrobe draped on a chair at the foot of the bed. Mom squeezed me so tight it hurt, but the hurt wasn't her grasp. I swallowed and held back my tears, for my mother's sake.

CHAPTER SIX

Tea at 5B

Rain splashed on the windowsill. I tucked the covers around me like a cocoon and curled inside them, loving the idea that it was going to be one of those lazy Sunday mornings when Mom read *The New York Times* while she ate cinnamon-raisin bagels with cream cheese and I stayed under the quilt an extra hour. Especially after the excitement of yesterday.

When Mom finally got up and went to the bathroom to take a shower, I raced over to the phone to call Jenny, waiting impatiently for her to answer. Would Jenny mind my news since she hadn't gotten her period yet?

"Guess what?" I blurted as soon as I heard her voice.

Tea at 5B

"What?" Jenny sounded as if her mouth was filled with food.

I took a deep breath. "I got my period yesterday afternoon."

Jenny began to cough as if she were choking.

"Are you all right?" I asked.

"Did I hear you say what I think you said? I can't believe the day you had. Madame Van Dam. Robby. And now this!"

"Oh, Jenny."

"Were you scared? Does it hurt, Allie? The truth."

Jenny didn't even like to get a scrape on her knee.

"Achey. Not like a stomachache after you've had too many French-fried onion rings. More like when Coach makes us touch our toes twenty times and do sit-ups until our backs and legs are killing us. And not even that exactly. At least that's what it is like for me. It's hard to explain."

"Well, I'll know what you mean one of these days. Do you feel the same? Cynthia Wellsley told Ariel Stone that she feels different."

"Remember the time when we flew up into the Girl Scouts and put away our Brownie uniforms for good?"

"It was great getting the new green dresses, wasn't it?"

"I know. And our mothers took us out that

night for ice cream at Pig-Out Heaven afterward," I said.

"And they let us stay up a hour past our bed-times, like adults."

"A little like that."

"Oh," Jenny said. "Like that."

Her voice sounded kind of distant. Not angry. Just weird.

"Do you want to come over this afternoon?" I asked, hoping she wasn't hurt or mad at me for something I couldn't prevent, or make happen.

"Let me ask." When Jenny came back to the telephone, she said, "Are you sure you're feeling up to me coming?"

"Jenny," I said, "don't be ridiculous."

"What time?"

"As soon as you can," I answered.

Great. Nothing had changed between us. I for-got to tell her about how I thought I had worms like her mutt Madge. That was worth a good laugh.

When I hung up, my mother came out of the shower, rubbing her hair briskly with a towel. "I bumped into Madame Van Dam on my way getting bagels this morning. I told her I needed to finish drawing her herbs up at her place. Would you like to tag along later today? You could play with her rabbit."

"Jenny's coming over. Can she come too?"

Tea at 5B

"I imagine it will be fine, but you never know with people. I'll have to call first." Mom tapped my nose playfully with the tip of her finger. "Feeling okay?"

"Not great. I've been better."

I looked down at her old lilac-and-blue-striped beach thongs that doubled as slippers—the ones she had bought the summer we went to Cape Cod the year Dad got sick. He agreed to take time off from work and not teach summer school for extra money like he always did.

"You'll be okay. My big girl." Mom hugged me. Her hair smelled of shampoo. "You'll always be my baby." She pinched my cheek. I groaned. "Just kidding."

But I knew she wasn't.

Jenny came for lunch. The three of us sat around the small table eating tuna fish sandwiches. Jenny seemed quiet. I think seeing me in person, knowing I had my period, was different than my telling her over the phone. After we were done, Jenny and I played some tapes and sang along while we took turns combing each other's hair. I re-braided Jenny's ponytail into a French braid. "I look so sophisticated," she kept saying in her Hollywood "dahling" accent as she admired herself in the mirror over my dresser.

We both applied crimson lipstick. Heartbreak Red. Thick and creamy.

THE FORTUNETELLER IN 5B

"*De*vine," Jenny said nasally, eyeing me as I pressed a tissue between my lips. "Simply luscious." She puckered hers together, staring at herself in the mirror. Then she closed her eyes and said to the air, "You'll always be mine."

"Forever, *mon amour*," I teased.

As she licked her lips, trying to make them seem glossier and fuller, Mom poked her head in the room. "Ready for tea, my dears? Your company is cordially requested."

"All of us?" I asked, kind of surprised.

Mom nodded. "Come, I've got work to do. It's not going to be only tea and crumpets upstairs."

"You're telling me," Jenny whispered as we revisited the scene of the crime: the very staircase we had spied on not too long ago.

After my mother knocked on the door, we could hear several latches being unlocked. My mother winked at us. Madame Van Dam slowly opened the door. A cool breeze drifted across the hallway as we entered. Tabitha was running free. She hopped toward a small hutch on the floor in the corner and took a sip of water from a bowl. Madame Van Dam placed a half-eaten apple slice on the wire mesh inside the cage. She looked at Tabitha and smiled. It was the first real smile I'd seen from her. Sort of the same kind my mother gave me when she was pleased with something I did.

Tea at 5B

Pinned to the wall near the hutch was a small photograph of a man and a woman. The man had a long, curled mustache. A mop of black hair reached his shoulders. He wore a patched vest— maybe made from pieces of old clothes from family members loved and remembered. The woman had beads around her neck, a strand around her fore- head, dangling earrings, and ribbons braided in her dark, flowing hair. Her eyes were deep and black like Madame Van Dam's. The background glowed; their faces seemed out of focus the way faces were in the old silent movies I'd sometimes seen at the museum.

"Those were my parents, Anca and Raoul. They performed in taverns and nightclubs all over Eastern Europe. My father played the violin. Liszt. Brahms. My mother danced." Madame Van Dam narrowed her eyes and leaned closer to the torn photo, its sepia edges frayed. Was she trying to remember them from a very long time ago? Some- times I tried to see my father's face in my mind. It was always clear in my dreams, at night, but began to fade in the daylight. Madame Van Dam sighed deeply. "The only picture I have of them. I'm lucky to have it." And she turned away.

"What a beautiful dress," my mother said, star- ing up at a colorful costume of hand-woven threads. "Was it your mother's?"

THE FORTUNETELLER IN 5B

Madame Van Dam stroked the tattered hem of the dress tilted on a hanger perched on a nail. Her hand brushed across a delicate necklace draped over a hook stuck into the molding.

"That was mine," she said wistfully. "The little that's left of my past." Again, she turned away. What past was that? And if it was so sad, why did she have these things around that made her remember?

Madame Van Dam parted a clear-glass-beaded curtain and walked between its ropes toward the stove. She lifted the heavy lid of a black iron pot and stirred with a wooden spoon.

"A cauldron," Jenny whispered. "What's that smell?"

"*Sarmale*. Stuffed cabbage." Madame Van Dam had overheard her.

The books we'd read said that psychics had more sensitive hearing than other people. Jenny glanced in my direction as if to say, *You see?*

"Well, it smells delicious." My mother sniffed the air.

Madame Van Dam put a fork inside the pot and cut off a small piece on a plate resting next to the burner. "It's sweetened chopped meat, rolled inside a large cabbage leaf." She motioned for us to come. We hesitated as though she were the witch in Hansel and Gretel, waiting to push us in the oven.

"Go." My mother gave me a nudge.

Tea at 5B

I politely took a bite. Jenny's face showed fear. Her expression turned to one of relief when she realized I was still alive.

Jars marked MEDICINAL HERBS and labeled with strange names like cardamom, cumin, anise, and arrowroot lined the shelves. "My herbs and spices," Madame Van Dam said. She swept her hand across the feathery tops of potted plants lined up on the windowsill under an eerie purple light. A string of garlic was tacked to the ceiling. It swung gently like an exotic jungle vine. Then Madame Van Dam pulled a stool from under the countertop toward my mother. "We have important business to attend to, right, girls?" She looked straight at me while my mother sat down, propped a drawing pad on her knees and began to sketch.

"We do?" Jenny grabbed my arm.

Madame Van Dam led us through a teeny alcove off the studio into a very large, dark, walk-in closet. I drew a deep breath. It smelled of cedar, musk, vanilla beans, and mothballs—unlike our linen closet, which smelled of sachets. She tugged at a string attached to a single light bulb. Then she draped a sheer red scarf over the bulb to cut off the glare. My eyes zoomed toward the center of the closet. A Persian carpet covered an enormous trunk. *The* trunk. Our missing trunk. The foreign labels were on the side. The same dents. Several

THE FORTUNETELLER IN 5B

wooden stools surrounded it. Jenny squeezed my wrist so hard, she nearly cut off the circulation.

Several candles in small red glasses were lined in a row beneath a shelf holding statues of saints. The sweet smell of incense inside a brass urn made me dizzy. Silver-framed holy pictures scattered on the wall were surrounded by artificial flowers like an altar. There was another shelf with books on telepathy, psychic healing, reincarnation, spiritualism, and astrology. On a chair made from a large barrel lay one book that said on the jacket cover *Gypsies: The Romany People.* Next to a dusty crock, Madame Van Dam pulled out a deck of cards—not the usual kind that Jenny and I played poker with, but cards with pictures on the back, of people. We huddled in a circle and she placed the deck on the trunk next to a crystal pyramid. "Shuffle them three times," she demanded.

After I followed her instructions, she took the deck from me, spreading ten cards out on top of the rug. The carpet's warm, scratchy surface bothered my knees as it rubbed against them.

"Laying the tarot cards in this way is called the Tree of the Kabala. The Kabala is a mystical interpretation of the Bible developed by a certain group of rabbis. In the diagram of these cards, the mystics imagined themselves ascending the tree. There are many methods of laying out and interpreting the cards."

Tea at 5B

Jenny put her hand on my knee. I could feel the sweat from her palm as Madame Van Dam let out a few "oo's" and "ah's."

"What do they say?" Jenny couldn't contain herself.

"*Şapte*," she said in another language. "Seven's a magical number."

"That's my lucky number!" I shouted. "I was born on the seventh of July, the seventh month of the year, at seven o'clock in the morning."

"A coincidence?" Jenny wondered aloud.

Madame Van Dam raised her hand. "Not according to me."

Jenny and I had our faces almost touching as we waited to see what card came up next.

"Oh, my God!" Jenny cried as I paled. Her fingernails dug into my skin, leaving deep red marks.

Madame Van Dam had laid down a card with a skeleton in a black-hooded robe holding a sickle.

"Sorry." Jenny shivered, removing her hand as we glared at the card. "What does it mean?" she asked for me as I looked away, pretending it wasn't there.

"The Death card can mean many things. Not all necessarily bad. The loss of a relative. A symbol of change. Rebirth—like a passage from one thing to the next. Death takes away, but it can also re-

THE FORTUNETELLER IN 5B

store. We can begin again. It can be a liberating card."

I didn't feel I could look at it that way at all. Death seemed final to me. The one thing that you couldn't change.

Madame Van Dam turned over some cards for Jenny. "Number nine."

Jenny stared at her, waiting for an explanation. "Yes?"

"A very lucky Gypsy number."

Jenny smiled, feeling blessed.

Thank God, I heard my mother's voice from the other side of the half-opened door, because I had had enough adrenaline for one afternoon. "Anyone home? I'm done." She peered around the door and came over to me, putting her hands on the back of my neck under my hair, slightly massaging me. "You're soaked," she said, touching a damp lock of my hair. I sighed with relief at having her next to me.

"Tea, anyone?" Madame Van Dam put the cards away in a box and went back into the studio.

"She's not going to read tea leaves, is she?" Jenny asked with excitement.

"I don't know," I said, still bothered about the Death card, even though Madame Van Dam had acted as if it were something good. Should I trust her?

Tea at 5B

The tea kettle whistled. Madame Van Dam poured boiling water over dry shredded leaves in a strainer. Then she filled each glass with this steaming colored water. Each glass was held in a bright copper holder, which was too hot to pick up. She sliced four pieces of apple strudel. "My mother used to give my younger sister and me this on Saturday nights after a show." She closed her eyes, breathing the aroma of the strong tea. Her lashes were thick like a zebra's.

"Does your sister live near you?" my mother asked.

"No." Madame Van Dam moved her plate aside.

"In another part of the country?" Jenny asked.

I kicked her under the table, tightening my lips.

"She died when she was very young."

"How terrible. I'm sorry for you." Mom put her hand on Madame Van Dam's arm. She seemed so far away; as if my mother, Jenny, and I were not here.

Madame Van Dam got up from the table and put her unfinished tea in the sink. "Be sorry for her and the life she never lived." As she washed her cup and plate, we quickly finished our strudel.

"Well," my mother said awkwardly after the silence, as she smoothed the creases in her blouse

THE FORTUNETELLER IN 5B

and stood up, "how can the girls and I thank you for a most unusual afternoon?"

Madame Van Dam smiled slightly.

I realized as we left that I hadn't brought any money to pay her for reading our cards. She hadn't taken any money for my palm reading, and I knew she'd never take payment for this either. Somehow, I'd have to repay her.

As soon as we got into my apartment and closed the door to my bedroom, Jenny burst out, "What do you think's in the trunk? And did you see that string of garlic? There was enough to supply an entire village in the Carpathian Mountains, home of you know which count—there's usually a run on blood when he's around. I wouldn't want her to do any volunteer work for the Red Cross."

"Jenny," I said, annoyed.

"What?"

"Nothing."

I decided to leave it alone. I felt peculiar about the afternoon. And how unhappy Madame Van Dam seemed when she talked about her sister. Why shouldn't she be? It was sad when people died before they'd done all the things that they wanted to do, and seen all the things that they should have seen.

CHAPTER SEVEN

Growing Up

Monday morning, while Mrs. Jackson was setting up a filmstrip called "Your Body and You," Jenny shoved a fortune from a Chinese cookie under my chin that read: *A shared experience in friendship.* "Is this timing or is this timing?" she asked. "Do you think it means what *I* think it means?"

"And what's that?"

"You know," she murmured, "that I'll get mine too. Soon."

"Could be." I smiled.

"Lights out." Mrs. Jackson motioned for Cynthia to flick the switch. "Time to learn about our bodies."

There was snickering in the back of the room when someone echoed "Our bodies?" while Cynthia whispered, "Mrs. Jackson's measurements look like they're 50-50-50. Looks like she developed ages ago and kept going."

We got to see cartoon drawings of different parts of the female anatomy and how babies grew inside. The girl on the screen had pigtails, which seemed odd since the filmstrip was showing maturation. Then we saw a short video with the cast from the Broadway show *Annie*. They spoke about what it felt like getting their periods. Most of them were around eleven and twelve when it happened, which made me feel funny inside for Jenny. Then I wondered how many girls in the sixth grade actually had theirs. Maybe Cynthia had been telling the truth for once, because when she waved her hand to ask a question, I saw some hair under her armpits. And I also had felt little stubbles of hair when her leg brushed up against mine in gym. Was her mother allowing her to shave her legs already?

Everyone giggled when the lights went back on and the boys tried to get into the room. "Come back in ten minutes." Mrs. Jackson pointed toward the door. Ten minutes! Is that all it took to tell us about the facts of life? She continued, "Here are some personal products you will need to know about during your time of maturing." There were all sorts of boxes lined up on a table. She was a few days too late for me. "Feel free to ask any questions." A hush came over the room. "Now I know how to get quiet," she said. We all laughed.

The only question came from Dana Valente. "Will I still be able to ride my horse in shows if I'm menstruating?"

Mrs. Jackson smiled in her nice motherly way. "Do what feels comfortable."

After Coach led the boys back into the classroom, no one made any eye contact during the whole math lesson until lunch. And then the lunchroom was noisier than usual.

While Jenny and I waited on line for the chilled fruit, she grabbed a container of milk and asked nonchalantly, "Did you learn anything new?"

"I guess." I shrugged. "Did you?"

"Sort of." She shrugged too.

Jenny probably felt as strange about this as I did.

Then she poked me in the side with a straw. Robby Berkert was two trays ahead of us getting the Twin Taco Surprise as we pushed along the metal track toward the cash register. I poked her back. "Stop it!" I cried. "He'll see you."

Robby turned around for the silverware and smiled. "He noticed you." Jenny pinched my arm.

"He's smiling at Larry Lastradinaro, not me."

"At you," she said firmly. "Smile back."

My jaw clenched. Did he think I was growling?

THE FORTUNETELLER IN 5B

I covered my mouth and felt a pimple emerging near my bottom lip. Great.

"Could you grab me an apple?" he yelled as Miss Todd, the cashier, impatiently waited for him to hand over his lunch ticket. I gave him the thumbs up sign and chose a shiny red one from the bin. "Toss it." He put his hands in the air, ready to catch.

"And it's mighty Pilaf pitching the first inning." Larry cupped his hands, sounding like an announcer. "Folks, I think she's about to show us her fast ball, the one that made her famous, placing her in the Baseball Hall of Fame alongside the greats."

I hesitated, and then hurled the apple in the air. It hit Robby square in the chest.

There wasn't a hole big enough for me to crawl into. I don't know who felt worse, him or me. I rushed ahead on line. "Are you okay? I'm really sorry. I'm better at soccer than baseball. I didn't mean it."

"I'd be worried if you did." Robby laughed as Larry pulled him by the arm.

"See you," I said, now feeling mortified about hitting Robby.

"See you." He walked toward the tables where the seventh graders ate.

Jenny ran up behind me. "What did he say?"

"I'm so embarrassed, I could die." I sat on the

Growing Up

long bench with the other sixth graders and I hid my head in my hands.

"You know he likes you."

"Jenny, he doesn't."

"He was drooling like Madge on a hot day in August."

"Touching. So romantic, Jen. Comparing Robby to a dog."

Jenny went on. "The potion is working. Can you imagine if you got one of his hairs? He'd be all over you like an ant in honey."

"Could we drop this?" I insisted, glancing up at the unpleasant sounds of Dana sipping the last drops of milk from the bottom of her container. She sounded like a herd of elephants drinking in one of those *Wild Asia* specials on TV.

"The next time you need help, write Dear Abby."

"I'll remember that."

She elbowed my side. "Only kidding."

We both tossed our garbage in the can and went into the playground. Cynthia and a few other girls were clustered near the swing set and giggled as we walked by. Jenny and I pretended not to hear them, but Cynthia had a smirk on her face a mile long. "Some of us were wondering if you two girls have grown up yet?" And they all began to laugh again as Cynthia accentuated the word *grown*.

THE FORTUNETELLER IN 5B

"I don't think that's anyone's business." I said.

"Because there's no *business* to tell," Cynthia shot back.

Everyone in the group clearly sided with Cynthia.

Dana added, "I bet neither of you has become a woman yet."

"You're so flat, Bolero, they could use you as a knock-hockey board."

I dug my fingers into Jenny's forearm to let her know without words *Be quiet*, and I pulled her away. "Why didn't you tell her? That you are, and I'm not," she said. "I feel so humiliated."

"People like that shouldn't make you feel bad. They're not worth it."

"You're a real friend, Allie," Jenny said as she looked up at a robin hopping from branch to branch in a tree, seeming interested in it, but I could see she was holding back her tears. It reminded me of the time I was the only Jewish kid on a soccer team. Mom had told Dad she overheard another parent commenting on it to a couple of mothers and fathers. "I'll sit with the other Jewish parents," Mom had said loudly. And she moved to the bleachers on the other side of the field, leaving the parents stunned. I remember my mother said that her anger didn't make her feel weak; it made her powerful. To do something about it.

CHAPTER EIGHT

Ouija Board

"Come over today after school," Jenny pleaded as the last bell rang and we loaded our backpacks with notebooks and stray pencils.

"You know my mother usually likes me to go straight home after school and do my homework."

Cynthia Wellsley passed us on the street near the crossing guard and acted as if nothing had happened. "Real sensitive," I muttered under my breath as Jenny's body tensed. "I'll come," I said to Jenny. I knew she needed me.

When Jenny opened the door to her apartment with her key, we were greeted by two very strange-looking people seated on folding chairs in the foyer. "Don't mind them." Jenny put her hand up to the side of her mouth. "Prospective clients. Mom's

THE FORTUNETELLER IN 5B

helping with the casting of a movie about killer slugs. Doesn't that man look sluglike?"

Off in the corner was some guy in a raincoat, fast asleep. "Uh-huh," I agreed.

He snorted as Mrs. Bolero came out of a small room off the center hall and lightly jostled him. He followed her, trailing slowly into her office. We overheard him say, "I was in 'Zom, Are You There?' and 'The Attack of the Fruit Fly.' In my most recent credit, I played a giant mole. The movie will be released this Halloween. It's called 'They Came from the Bronx, Part II.' "

"He's a natural," Jenny cooed as I glanced over at a woman with a stole wrapped around her shoulders. The head of a dead animal dangled at the end. "Another sure candidate for the role," she said.

"Isn't she hot in that? It's spring." I felt totally grossed out.

"Who said she's alive?" Jenny giggled, pulling me into her bedroom past her cello, which leaned against an old upright piano. It was like the one we sold after Dad died and we had to move into our one-bedroom apartment.

Mom had said, "The space is too tight. We'll buy another piano, maybe, someday."

Would I have been up to Chopin and Bach if we hadn't sold the piano? Like Jenny was on the cello?

Jenny tossed frilly throw pillows onto her white

Ouija Board

wicker rocker and bounced on her mattress, sprawling herself out. "My mother always says, 'These people are colorful.' Madame Van Dam would fit right in. She might even be boring compared to what drags in here."

"You didn't think so this weekend."

"True, veddy true, my dear." Jenny batted her lashes.

The bamboo shade was rolled up to the top of the window. I stared at the brick building across the street. A calico cat was sitting on a high ledge. It hunched its back when it began to drizzle and tiptoed inside an open window. The sky blackened, and there was a sudden storm.

"I've got a great idea!" Jenny jumped off the bed and stood on a stepstool in her closet. From the top shelf, she lifted down a Ouija board.

"If you're going to ask all sorts of questions about you-know-who in the seventh grade, then forget it."

Jenny placed her hand on the board. "Actually, I was going to find out who or what Madame Van Dam really is," she said. She balanced the board on our knees between us as we sat cross-legged on her bed. We closed our eyes and slid a small triangular pointer across the board. "Let's ask simple questions first." Jenny seemed to push the pointer toward me.

THE FORTUNETELLER IN 5B

"Don't lean on it," I said firmly.

"I'm not," Jenny whined.

I took a deep breath. "Okay. Will Jenny be in my seventh-grade homeroom class next year?"

As the pointer went around in a random motion our bodies swayed. Suddenly, the pointer stopped. I opened my eyes. Jenny's were already open. It was resting on the letters *C* and *D*, pointing to the word *Yes*.

"Great!" Jenny yelled. "Now it's my turn." We started in a circular pattern, zooming past the words MYSTIFYING ORACLE and TALKING BOARD SET, over all the letters in the alphabet. "Does R. B. like Allie?"

"You promised!" I shouted, dropping my fingers from the tip of the Ouija disk into my lap.

"All right. A different subject. Is Madame Van Dam a witch?"

Once again our fingers zipped across the board, flying past pictures of the sun and the moon. We paused between the words YES and NO.

"Is she a vampire?" Jenny continued.

Again, we remained between the two words, unanswered.

"Maybe that's not her *real* name?" Jenny suggested.

"I've wondered." I said. "Is that Madame Van

Ouija Board

Dam's real name?" The Ouija stopped, sort of near NO. "Did you force it?"

"Are you calling me a cheater?" Jenny asked, stopping, and then starting to rotate the pointer again. I joined in the flow of her movement.

I repeated, "Does Madame Van Dam have a different name?"

The disk made a straight-arrowed path to YES.

"What's the first initial of her real name?" Jenny was excited.

We peered through the clear plastic bubble over the letter *S*.

"I can't believe this," I moaned. "You think it has powers?"

"Shh," Jenny said. "What's her last name?" The pointer didn't move. Then the Ouija jutted to the edge of the board next to the words SALEM, MASS, U.S.A. "I rest my case." Jenny looked smug. "That's where all the witches were burned at the stake during the Puritan times. And," Jenny pointed, raising her eyebrows, "that's also where this board is made. So maybe it knows some answers." Then she blurted, "How old will I be when I get my period?"

As if by gravitational pull, we headed for the word *Good-bye*.

I felt quiet inside. Jenny looked at me. "Should we put it away?" I said, touching Jenny's knee. "Or do you want to try again?"

THE FORTUNETELLER IN 5B

"Some other time," Jenny said, placing the Ouija board back in its box. I hugged her. Then she took a wad of pink rubbery stuff from the top of her headboard. "Want some gum?" she asked, trying to change her mood.

"Eech!" I gave her a punch and she handed me a fresh piece.

Jenny and her mother had gotten free tickets for the opening of some horror film. They dropped me off in a cab on their way. Mrs. Pearlstein was in the hall dusting a mirror when I let myself in. "Darling," she said, "wipe your feet off on the mat." It was already damp from a pair of wet, muddy sneakers resting on it. Probably my downstairs neighbor Andrew's.

"I didn't forget the money I owe you, Mrs. Pearlstein."

"Don't worry yourself. I know you're a responsible young lady. You'll give me when you're ready. Maybe you want to earn a little? It couldn't hurt."

"How?" I looked at her curiously.

"Vacuuming the carpet in the halls one day. Dusting the mirrors and wall sconces at each landing. The banisters too."

"Sure." Now I wouldn't have to ask Mom to advance my allowance or look for a baby-sitting job.

Ouija Board

Everyone thought I was still a little too young to take care of children, even though I didn't think so. And the only dog I knew to walk was Madge, and Jenny had to do that for free. But most of all, it would give me an opportunity to be on the fifth floor. Without spying. A legitimate reason.

That night, when I was cuddling with my mother, I told her about my job. She looked pleased but stated, "Don't let it interfere with any schoolwork."

"It's just for a couple of times."

"Well, that's good. I'm glad to see you're industrious."

"Like you, Ma."

"You always know how to get on my good side."

Then I said, "We saw a video this morning with the cast of 'Annie' about growing up."

Mom faced me on the pillow we were sharing. "Our lessons were called 'Hygiene.' We saw a black-and-white filmstrip describing manners. A doofy-looking boy in a crew cut with glasses, wearing a plaid short-sleeved shirt, and a girl in a flip hairdo, shirtwaist dress, and bobby socks were in a scene to show us the right way to handle a first date and the first kiss. The boy is supposed to make the first move, they said. And the wrong way—was when the girl is aggressive. I guess I didn't learn too much, because I kissed your father first." Mom laughed.

"You kissed Dad *first*?"

THE FORTUNETELLER IN 5B

"Right on his sideburn. I was seventeen, sitting next to him while he was driving in his powder blue Impala convertible. He looked so cute when we stopped at a traffic light." I closed my eyes, tight, trying to imagine my mother and father that young together. "Dad was my type."

"How did you know?"

"You just know. It feels right. Inside."

Robby was my type too. Then for some reason I thought of Jenny. It made me feel funny, like I had passed her in a race, and she was a friend. It didn't seem right.

"Ma? I think Jenny feels sad that I got my period, and she didn't get hers yet."

"Oh." A smile broadened across my mother's face. "You sure it's not you who's feeling sad for her?" And she brushed my hair off my forehead. "My best friend, Janice Ehler, developed before I did. The boys really liked her, and I felt left out of a world she had entered before me. At the time, we drifted apart because she started going to a lot more parties than I did. Looking back, I see that everyone catches up. Let me tell you a story. When you were two, our next-door neighbor's baby was already speaking and toilet trained. I wondered if anything was wrong with you. And your father said, 'Lorna, by the time they go to college, they're all toilet trained.' I stopped worrying. And you see. It worked! You're not even in junior high yet." Mom and I laughed. "Jenny and you will be fine."

"We'll stay friends? Always? Forever?" I asked.

"Who can predict the future? I don't have a crystal ball."

"Madame Van Dam does. Wouldn't it be wonderful if it were real?"

"I'm not so sure," Mom said.

"Why?"

"Half the excitement of life, if not all, is the not knowing. The adventure of trying to get where each of us wants and hopes to go. It would be like reading the ending of a book on the first page. Dreams are an important part of life." My mother kissed me on the cheek and slipped out from beneath the cover, tucking it around my body as though I were little again. "I'm always going to love you. *That's* forever."

"I love you, Mom. I'm glad you're my mother."

Moonlight danced on my quilt. I sank my head deeper into my pillow. Should I have asked the Ouija board how Dad was? Wasn't it supposed to give messages from departed loved ones? Maybe Mom was right, and some things should be kept for endings? Unknown. There was a part of me that still wanted to ask the Ouija board, Dad, are you okay? And have the disk point without faltering to *Yes*.

CHAPTER NINE

My Two Neighbors

Mrs. Pearlstein was rattling some garbage cans next to the stoop when I came home from school. "Alley cats," she said, "trying to get into the trash. What a mess." She fastened the bent lids tighter. "So, do I have a helper today? I'm off this afternoon from the antique store."

I quickly calculated how much homework I had and said, "Yes."

"Put your books away. Here's a *schmatteh*, and we're in business."

I took the rag from Mrs. Pearlstein, ran upstairs, and threw my backpack on the kitchen table. There was a note scribbled, tagged to the refrigerator: *Had to run to the Botanical Society. Will be*

My Two Neighbors

back around five. Love, Mom. P.S. Do your homework!

"I will!" I shouted to the air, slamming the door behind me.

Bottles of spray cleaners and old ripped-up terry-cloth towels were lined on the bench in the front hall. "In your school clothes?" Mrs. Pearlstein tapped her foot on the rug a few times.

I looked down at my skirt and top. "Don't worry. They have to be washed anyway."

"Don't say I didn't warn you."

"I won't." I smiled.

"We'll start at my floor and work our way up?"

"Sure." I wondered if Madame Van Dam was at home. I had counted on doing this by myself.

Mrs. Pearlstein put a little lemon oil on a dust-cloth. I did the same, smoothing it over the banister. The grains in the wood deepened to a dark brown with each swirl of the rag. "I used to do this with my mother," Mrs. Pearlstein said. "In our house in Boro Park. Brooklyn."

"Is that where you were born?" I asked.

She threw her head back and laughed. "Poland. Bialystok."

"Like in bagels and bialys?"

"Yes." She laughed again.

"How old were you when you came to America?"

"One. I was quarantined the whole trip. Mea-

THE FORTUNETELLER IN 5B

sles. They wouldn't even let my parents see me. I guess the people in charge were afraid of everyone on the boat getting it. An epidemic."

"Your parents must have been very brave to leave their home."

"Brave." She threw her arms in the air. "A suitcase and what you could carry. Brave," she repeated. "Yes, they were brave. There was also no choice. We left for the same reasons Jews always leave. No one wanted us. This time it was Russian cossacks. The soldiers swept through the Jewish quarters on their horses. They beat and massacred the people. It was called pogroms. My parents hid in a cellar, or so the story goes. And there were dogs, too. Searching. Like howling wolves. To this day, I don't like dogs. Especially big ones. The local police were blamed for what the cossacks did, so they weren't good to the Jews after that. Oh, the scapegoating that goes on. The hatred. After several years my parents had enough, and they left."

"It's a good thing."

"Good? Yes it was good. Those who lived through that and stayed lived to die later of starvation in the ghettos during World War II, or were sent off to be gassed in concentration camps. A lot of my family stayed, and died. They were deported to the Treblinka death camp." Mrs. Pearlstein's hardened expression softened as she touched my hair.

My Two Neighbors

"My hair was auburn like yours. Red hair was a dead giveaway that you were Jewish."

"What?" I said. "Sometimes people think I'm Irish, with my reddish brown hair and freckles."

"Not in blond-haired Poland and Germany and Austria." Mrs. Pearlstein held her hand up to her chest. "Not in Eastern Europe in nineteen thirty-nine."

"Mrs. Pearlstein?"

"I'm fine, darling. I was just remembering being a child. My parents spoke mostly Yiddish. I didn't even speak English until I started school. Safe, in Brooklyn, I still used to ask myself at night where would I hide if the Germans came to take me away? Here, in America." She shook her head. "I always thought under a big old rolltop desk in my parents' basement. Sometimes I'd crawl into a corner beneath it in the dark, sit curled up very still, and try not to breathe, practicing for the time if, God forbid, it happened again. As if that would save me. What a foolish child." She sounded hoarse, and put her dustcloth down at her side.

"Would you like me to finish up?" I asked.

"That would be nice." She strained a faint smile.

As I worked my way upstairs, I couldn't put out of my mind all that Mrs. Pearlstein had told me. What would I take if I had only one suitcase to pack? I'd have to leave my favorite stuffed caterpillar, the one Dad gave me when I was five. That was too big. I felt a longing inside already. I'd take the cloisonné pin Mom let me have. I'd wear it. Some of my favorite books; I'd keep rereading them. Warm clothes. A toothbrush. Toothpaste. How long would that last? I always wasted so much. Dad hated the way I squeezed in the middle of the tube. Oh, a cassette of me singing songs when I was three, and my father reciting the poem "Father William," by Lewis Carroll. Us playing the piano together. Then I'd have to take the tape recorder, too. Would that make too much noise? The birthday card my mother made for me on Japanese rice paper with pressed flowers when I turned seven. A pencil portrait she did of me at eight. My Brownie uniform. No, I'd have to leave that. This was horrible. All the picking and choosing. It was like when we had to sell the piano. A girl younger than me was starting lessons. She came with her parents to our old house. I knew that Dad's fingers had touched those ivory keys, and now it would be in some stranger's place, them using my piano, sitting on the bench he and I sat on. Now I knew how it felt. Only a little. I couldn't even begin to possibly know what it really felt like. I brushed away a tear with my sleeve, and my eyes stung. I found myself alone on the fifth floor.

My Two Neighbors

It was still. Quiet. The afternoon sun streamed through the skylight above the ladder to the roof. I twisted a fresh cloth around the carved spindles under the rail, rubbing them with such intensity that I didn't hear Madame Van Dam come up the steps. She surprised me when I heard her put the key in her door. I turned around and looked up. She stared into my eyes. Piercing. That was the word for her eyes. Like they could see right through me. Could she? Was it my imagination?

"I'm only cleaning," I said, still feeling guilty for the time I spied on her apartment with Jenny.

"Yes, I see. Would you like to rest and have some tea?"

Tea, alone, with Madame Van Dam. In 5B. I could be brave. This was nothing, right, compared to the decisions people had to make? "Thank you," I said, placing the rag next to the bottle of oil on the ladder. She held the door as I followed her inside.

Shoeboxes filled with different-colored spools of thread, ribbons, zippers; an old metal candy can of stray buttons in various shapes and sizes; cloth scraps were scattered across the dining-room table. A pin cushion shaped like a strawberry lay on the floor next to a large dressmaker's dummy, the kind I saw at the tailor shop in the dry-cleaning store. An ancient-looking shiny black Singer sewing ma-

THE FORTUNETELLER IN 5B

chine with delicate gold flowers scrolled near a tiny lightbulb rested on top of a heavy mahogany cabinet. A dress was tucked firmly under the needle, sewn midway, left undone. It was a satin gown, the type an actress might wear in a gangster movie. A plastic organizer mounted on the open door of the sewing cabinet separated thimbles, snaps, needles of different sizes, embroidery thread, and chalk. Several bolts of fabric were draped across the love seat in the nearby living-room area.

Madame Van Dam eyed my every move as she put up the pot of tea. I noticed her necklaces draped around her neck as she took off her cape.

"They're pretty," I said.

"Venetian glass beads mixed with turquoise and coral."

The beads glistened and fell through her fingers as she lifted the strands, rippling like waves. "Come," she said, "I have something to show you."

From on top of another cabinet, she lifted a wooden tray divided by tiny compartments filled with shells of different shapes and colors. Then she carefully spread some across her lap, holding her knees together so they wouldn't fall down. "A *ghioc*. Cowry shell. Shells of certain sea animals that were used for money, like coins, off the coast of Africa and in parts of southern Asia. Take a shell. It's yours."

My Two Neighbors

"Are you sure?"

She placed a shell in my hand. "Maybe you will need it someday to buy something special." And she grinned at me mischievously.

Then she swooped up the shells in the folds of her skirt, using it like a satchel, and placed them one by one back in the tray.

We had tea on the only clear space in the apartment—the countertop near Tabitha's hutch. I patted her as I walked by. Above was the photograph of Madame Van Dam's parents pinned to the wall. The one thing I forgot to list: family pictures. Especially the one of me, Mom, and Dad on a sand dune in Cape Cod—the water surrounding us as if we were on our own island that last summer all together. How many photos could I stuff inside one suitcase, and albums of vacations and birthday parties, alongside socks and underpants and sturdy shoes? How did anyone decide between the things they wanted and the things they needed to survive?

At night, while I was brushing my teeth and Mom was casually watching me from the hall, I asked, "Where were all my grandparents born?"

"First, spit out the toothpaste," she said, as it foamed around my mouth like a rabid dog. "Why the question now?"

"Just because," I said, wondering why I had never thought of asking it before.

THE FORTUNETELLER IN 5B

"On Dad's side, Grandpa came from Lithuania. Now it's part of Russia. Grandma was born here in Manhattan. And on my side, Mama and Papa came from Poland."

"Oh." I was surprised. "Like Mrs. Pearlstein."

"You were talking to Mrs. Pearlstein about where she was born?"

I nodded. "She came from Bialystok."

"Interesting. My parents were from Lodz."

"Why did they come here?"

Mom gave a dry laugh. "For the same reason the Pilgrims came to America. Religious persecution. Thank God, my parents left years before the Holocaust."

"Or else you and I wouldn't be here. We wouldn't exist."

"Bite your tongue," Mom said, like her mother when she didn't want me saying out loud what I had just said.

"It's true," I whispered.

"Probably," she said, drawing me close to her.

"I'm glad they came here, then." I sighed.

"So am I." She kissed the top of my head and swung her arm around my waist. "Let's have some hot chocolate with whipped cream."

"Sounds good." And I swung my arm around her waist too.

CHAPTER TEN

Mother's Day

Sunday was Mother's Day. At breakfast I gave my mother her gift. She pushed aside her French toast and tugged at the gold thread tied around dried pink baby's breath that I had placed in the center on top of the box. As she lifted the tissue paper, her eyes widened. "Alex! You shouldn't have." Mom rotated the Chinese snuff bottle, resting it in the palm of her hand, examining the painted twigs and blossoms.

"Do you like it?"

"No, I love it!" She hugged me. "Sweetie, you went all out."

"I'm glad you like it, Ma. I figured it would go nicely in front of your drawing table. You could

THE FORTUNETELLER IN 5B

look up from your work every once in a while and stare at someone else's."

"That's a lovely idea." My mother carefully propped it on the windowsill next to a bright green ceramic frog I had made in first grade. She ran her hand across the frog's smooth glazed surface. "Of course your sculpture will always have a larger place in my heart." Mom put the gold thread inside the box, which she saved next to her brushes and drawing pencils. "Let's do something special today. We'll walk to the Boat House, sit in the park, and go out for an early dinner. How does that sound?"

"Great," I said, helping her clear off the table. Could it be great without Dad? "I'll be dressed in a minute." I went into my room and threw on a jogging outfit. When I came out, my mother was putting on her eyeliner. I watched her brush her long brown hair into a ponytail, tying a blue velvet ribbon around the elastic band.

"Not so bad for a forty-year-old." She pressed her lips together and applied some gloss.

"Not *too* bad," I teased.

"Why, you!" We chased each other around the couch. "Truce!" she shouted. "Okay, I admit it— I'm not as young as I used to be."

"You look good, Ma."

She smiled and fastened her belted change purse around her waist. "I'm ready. Let's go."

Mother's Day

Madame Van Dam was coming down the staircase as Mom was closing the door to our apartment. Tabitha was in a harness. I knelt down to scratch her behind the ears. Her nose twitched. Suddenly she hopped in the air, and then stretched out like a rug on the floor. Madame Van Dam adjusted the leash and said, "Happy Mother's Day."

I think my mother was about to say, "You, too," when she stopped herself. "Do you have any children?"

Madame Van Dam shook her head no. She glanced down at Tabitha and smiled at her sniffing the toe of my sneaker. "I was going to take her to Central Park for some exercise."

"We're heading in that direction too. Would you like to join us?" Mom looked at me as if to say, Is that all right? I smiled, and with my eyes tried to show yes.

"Tabitha, would you like to go to the park with these nice neighbors?" Madame Van Dam spoke to her as though she were a person. Tabitha pulled at the leash.

We began to walk toward Central Park West. Tabitha's ears flopped around like a cocker spaniel's when she turned her head and swiftly hopped across the sidewalk. Children followed, pointing their chubby fingers. A man with a Snugli tied around his chest bent down. "Can my baby touch her fur?"

THE FORTUNETELLER IN 5B

The baby looked as though he were going to grab Tabitha's soft fluffy tail. Madame Van Dam backed away in time, protecting her.

I whispered to my mother, "Madame Van Dam is getting a lot of attention with her rabbit. Do you think she likes that?"

My mother raised her eyebrows. "People have many sides to them. Maybe she's more private than shy."

A man on the corner wearing a striped poncho and selling flowers waved to Madame Van Dam as we strolled by. She waved back. He motioned for her to come over and tossed a bunch of daisies in her large beaded satchel. When we got to a wooden bench and sat down, she handed my mother one. My mother twirled it as we quietly gazed at the rowboats skimming the water in the lake. Tabitha munched on long strands of onion grass and wild strawberries under the big oak tree shading us like an umbrella. Families strolled by. One family stopped and laid out a picnic on an old quilt. The mother rested her head on the father's lap. He stroked her hair as the children tossed a beach ball. Dad loved going to Jones Beach, making picnics of pot roast sandwiches, even having them on the boardwalk in the winter. "Food tastes better out-doors," he always said.

My mother looked down near her feet. "Look

Mother's Day

what I've done!" Scattered around her red leather sandals were small white petals, which she had torn off one by one from the daisy Madame Van Dam had given her. Mom tried to mash them in the dirt as if to erase them. She wiped the corner of her eye as she gazed dreamily at the family nearby.

Madame Van Dam leaned down, grabbed another daisy, and placed it in my mother's palm.

"I miss him today. Some days are better than others." Mom blotted her eyes again. They were red and puffy.

"He's watching over you," Madame Van Dam said comfortingly. "Loss is painful. I know." She looked away.

I stared at my mother. Then at Madame Van Dam. So she did know about Dad after all. I glanced at the petals on the ground. What kind of flowers were at my father's funeral? Were there any? My mind was completely blank about the cemetery. Afterward, there were baskets sent to the apartment of shiny waxen fruit and floral arrangements with lots of daisies and little cards tucked in expressing words of sympathy from people I had never heard of. And the day before, Ma picked out one of Dad's good suits that he wore on special occasions, the one she thought he looked so handsome in. It probably didn't fit. Too big from all the weight he had lost. Did they actually put it on? The rest of his

THE FORTUNETELLER IN 5B

clothes Mom donated to the Salvation Army before the year was up. Except that one flannel shirt.

Mom looked at me, and then spoke softly to Madame Van Dam. "My husband gave me a bouquet of daisies the day Alexandria was born." She closed her eyes, tight. A grin grew across her face. "Spring filled that room. I felt as if no one in the entire world existed except the three of us." Mom put her arm around me and leaned her head on my shoulder for just a moment. I kissed her cheek. Her skin was soft like peach fuzz.

After several silent minutes, Madame Van Dam dipped into her large satchel and pulled out an ordinary deck of cards. "Let's see how lucky we all are." She spread them out on a sheer scarf that she pulled from her bag the way a magician plucks endless scarves from his sleeve. She pointed to a series of cards and said in a hushed tone, "They're all red. Sunlight will fill your days, and the days of those close to you."

"Good going, Ma."

Mom elbowed me in the side to quiet me, since it seemed Madame Van Dam took this stuff very seriously.

Madame Van Dam felt the cards as though they were alive. Her long turquoise-and-silver earrings jangled. "I'm picking up vibrations. You have a good aura."

Mother's Day

"What's that?" I asked.

"A special light atmosphere surrounding your mother," she said, "invisible to us, but visible to the cards. That's why certain ones turn up. Like this two of hearts." She shifted the card toward my mother. "Love is in your future."

I didn't know whether to smile or not. Was there a twinkle in Mom's eye? Why? Didn't she love Dad? What was that whole story about the daisies when I was born? I realized that I didn't feel like smiling. I got up to stretch, kicking a few small pebbles as I made my way toward Tabitha. I looked back. "Can I take her for a walk?" Madame Van Dam nodded as she continued to read my mother's fortune.

"She's just some stupid fortuneteller," I said to Tabitha as we walked away. Now I was talking to a rabbit. Tabitha stared at me as though she were listening. Her eyes seemed almost black like Madame Van Dam's. Gypsy eyes, my mother called them. Tabitha headed for a winding path below a small cliff. A man held out his hand to help a woman balance as she gingerly made her way from one rock to another. She looked a lot older than my mother. The man was wearing a baby blue short-sleeved polo, the same kind my father wore when he did one of his projects around the apartment, like stripping paint from the wood moldings or building

THE FORTUNETELLER IN 5B

Mom's drafting table. When they paused and found a flat surface, he wrapped his hand around hers.

I thought of Grandma and Grandpa sitting on their beach chairs in Florida, a honeysuckle bush behind them—the one they planted when I was three. They bought me my own spade to help them dig. I could almost smell the honeysuckle's sweet perfume through the air as I closed my eyes, remembering how I once caught a glimpse of Grandma slipping her hand slowly into Grandpa's, cradled in his palm. She didn't suddenly jerk it away when she saw me watching as grown-ups often do when they feel caught in an act meant only for them. It was as though she wanted me to know it was okay to feel that way even when you're old. A lump came to my throat as I realized I would never see my mother and father that way. There would never be a photograph like the one on Grandma's dresser, of her and Grandpa celebrating their silver wedding anniversary.

Madame Van Dam and my mother were all packed up and waiting for me when I got back to the bench. "We're ready to go." My mother smoothed her hand down mine. Madame Van Dam took the leash from me and followed Tabitha's lead. We started to walk home.

"Mom, do you miss Dad very much?"

She let out a deep sigh. "At night. There's no

one to turn to and say, 'What do you think about our daughter getting 100 percent on her math test? Didn't she look mature the other day in her olive green dress?' Or, 'I'm going to pull my hair out if she doesn't straighten up that mess in her room.' "

"I miss Sunday mornings, when I'd come in your bedroom and cuddle between you and Dad in a sandwich hug."

"An open-faced sandwich isn't so bad, is it?" Mom squeezed my shoulder. "I'm glad I have you."

"I'm glad I have you too, Ma. Who else am I going to look at mold cultures and shrimp slides with, or talk to about growing up?"

Her eyes welled up with tears. I didn't say the usual "I love you." She just knew it. From that one look she gave me, I knew I was lucky to have her, and I couldn't imagine living in the world without her. It scared me because I knew someday I'd have to.

"Happy Mother's Day, Ma," I said.

"Thanks, darling."

"I'll race you home!" I yelled, running backward, facing her.

"Cheater!" she called after me as I took a head start.

I heard her keeping up, close behind.

"Some people will do anything to win," my mother gasped for breaths as she slid next to me

THE FORTUNETELLER IN 5B

on the front stoop. I was panting too. We waited for Madame Van Dam, off in the distance. A lumpy black mound was scurrying closer. "Should we invite Madame Van Dam to go out to eat? She's all alone today."

"She's pretty much alone everyday, except when she has those strange customers."

"It's my way of thanking her for letting me draw the herbs."

"Sure. Why not? Invite her."

Tabitha bounced up to me and nuzzled her nose into my palm, licking the salt from my sweaty fingertips.

"Would you like to go out to eat with us?" my mother asked Madame Van Dam. "Nothing fancy, just the little Italian place up the block."

"Can I take you to someplace different on the Lower East Side? A Rumanian steak house."

"Sounds interesting. I've never eaten at a Rumanian restaurant."

"We've probably eaten food from every nationality except that," I said.

"There are dishes from my country, and music, singing, lots of noise."

"I'll bring my earplugs," Mom said cheerfully. "We'll meet you downstairs at four. Is that too early? I thought before the crowds come."

Mother's Day

"That restaurant is always packed. It's like a continuous wedding. Don't be surprised if someone takes a forkful of food from your plate. That's how close the tables are."

"I'm prepared." Mom winked at me as we went to our apartment and Madame Van Dam returned to hers.

My mother took another one of her long, hot baths as I read a magazine article about how to have thin thighs in ten days. Why did I get a feeling this place from the Old Country didn't serve fruit salad?

At four o'clock Mom and I waited outside, watching people go by the brownstone. The sun was still beating on the pavement. A cool breeze blew through my mother's hair. Mom placed her hands around her waist above a pine green suede belt. Although I missed my father, I realized at this moment that seeing my mother alone all dressed up and looking so pretty hurt more than being without him, because where was Dad to see her? So maybe I had no right to be angry at Madame Van Dam's cards saying "Love is in your future" if that made my mother's eyes twinkle.

Madame Van Dam swooshed out the front door, the same way she had swooshed in on that first night we met. A whirlwind of activity seemed to surround her, even when nothing special was happening. Maybe it was her aura. She wore a turban with a feather in it that tickled my nose as she passed me on the stoop.

"We're ready," Mom said. "Shall we go?' Madame Van Dam swooped her hand in the direction of the street, and several heavy gold bracelets clanged together up and down her arm.

We followed like obedient children to the train station on 72nd Street, taking a downtown local.

The Rumanian steak house looked like a little hole in the wall from the outside. It looked the same inside, too. "Where are we?" I whispered to my mother as some man escorted us to a table under a loudspeaker next to an accordionist. I squeezed into a wooden chair shoved back to back with a stranger's. Business cards, yellowing with age, wallpapered the sides of the small dining room. Scotch-taped next to my seat was a card that said YONKEL'S BUTCHER SHOP: THE MAVEN OF MEATS.

My mother laid her hand on mine. "Treat this as an adventure."

"For our next rhapsody, a *doina*!" the accordionist bellowed into the microphone.

A heavyset woman wobbled up to the microphone. Amidst the noise I heard her say, "I would like to sing to you a beautiful melancholy folk song of love from my Rumanian homeland."

Mother's Day

Our waitress wiped her hands on a dish towel wrapped around her waist and tossed three laminated menus on the small square table. She disappeared as quickly as she had appeared while I watched the singer place her hands near her heart on her enormous chest, thrust them toward the microphone, and then return them to her chest. If Jenny were here, I knew I wouldn't have been able to keep a straight face. I still couldn't, without her, so I stared at a musician in an embroidered vest as he wove his way through the tables bowing his violin. When the singer broke into another melody, mostly everyone stopped eating and began to clap. Two old women danced with each other in the narrow aisle between a few tables next to the kitchen. The waitresses dashed in and out of the swinging doors, making their way around the dancers as they held heavy trays of food. Suddenly, my mother was swept up by a man in a folk dance with several other people. Madame Van Dam was pulled in too, until almost the entire restaurant was dancing. Even some of the kitchen help joined in. I watched my mother's hair flow, her cheeks flush as she snapped her fingers in the air. Napkins waved like flags in the wind. The tempo got wilder until everyone was in a frenzy. When the music stopped, Madame Van Dam and my mother slumped in their seats, exhausted.

THE FORTUNETELLER IN 5B

"I haven't danced like that," my mother's voice trailed off between gasps of air, "in years."

"Neither have I," Madame Van Dam admitted.

I was surprised to see Madame Van Dam in a way I never imagined her: carefree.

Our waitress returned. "Okay"—she flipped the other orders back on her small green pad—"what'll it be?"

"Do you have any hamburgers?" I begged, passing by the broiled chicken livers and sweetbreads, which I knew for a fact were the thymus glands.

She rolled her eyes, looking at Madame Van Dam as if to say, Where did you find this kid?

"Why don't you try the chopped tenderloin?" Madame Van Dam suggested. "It's like hamburger."

"And you?" the waitress turned to my mother.

"Chicken fricassee."

The waitress shook her head. "Not today. Get the broiled veal chops smothered with minced garlic. You won't be disappointed."

Garlic, I thought. Garlic was all over the menu with almost every dish. Jenny would have had a field day with her accusations after reading it.

The waitress stared at Madame Van Dam. "The usual? *Karnatzlack?*"

In especially bold type the menu said: FOR GARLIC EATERS ONLY.

Mother's Day

"What's that?" I shouted over the very loud music.

"Ground grilled sausage," the waitress answered impatiently.

Madame Van Dam handed her back the menu. "And the *patcha*," she added, turning toward me, "garlic-scented calf's foot jelly."

I crinkled my nose, longing for plain American food.

Mom patted my hand. "I'm just going to freshen up after that dance. Be right back, sweetie."

I felt awkward being left alone, here, with Madame Van Dam. I thought of following my mother to the ladies' room, but Madame Van Dam cleared her throat and looked directly at me. "I'd like to enter into a business arrangement with you."

First Mrs. Pearlstein, now her.

"Sure," I said politely, thinking this should be payment for the palm reading and crystal-ball gazing. What if it were some psychic experiment, and I learned I was five hundred years old?

"I'm going away for a week. Would you like to take care of Tabitha? You'd go upstairs and feed her, change the newspaper in the tray under her hutch, clean out her litter pan, and give her fresh water. And, of course, play with her. She needs attention. Do you think you could do that each day after school?"

THE FORTUNETELLER IN 5B

Why did I say sure? The idea of being all alone in 5B sent chills up my spine. Though Mom would be downstairs. And I'd ask Jenny to help.

"Sure," I repeated.

"Wonderful. That's settled."

"What's settled?" Mom asked, returning to the table.

"I'm going to take care of Tabitha for a week," I said. "Madame Van Dam is going away."

"Rabbit-sit." Mom chuckled.

Then I wondered, Where was Madame Van Dam going? Neither Mom nor I asked. I guess if she wanted to tell us, she would.

CHAPTER ELEVEN

Rabbit-sitting

When I called up Jenny to ask her to help me out with Tabitha, her father answered the phone. Jenny was practicing her cello in the background. Dad and I used to play a duet of "Chopsticks" with me always doing the higher octave.

"Hi," I said when she got on. "You'll never guess who I spent Mother's Day with."

"Let me take a wild stab at it. Your mother?"

"Cute, Jen. Yeah, my mother. And Madame Van Dam."

"How did she get into the picture?"

"My mom asked her. Anyway, we went to this Rumanian place that reminded her of 'the Old Country.' " I said it with a heavy accent. "And she asked me if I would take care of her rabbit this week while she goes away. Would you help me?"

"Why not? Maybe then we'll find out more about your mysterious neighbor. I just hope that this isn't like the movie 'Abbott and Costello Meet Frankenstein.' "

Monday afternoon after school, I waited for Jenny outside in the school yard. Robby Berkert was with a group of kids, and he was talking to Lindsay Blum, another seventh grader. She twisted a lock of long blond hair around her finger as he stood next to her, bouncing his new pink Spaulding ball. Lindsay had just had her ears pierced, and she was showing everyone her new pearl studs. I don't think Robby even noticed me watching as they walked off into Tutti-Fruiti for ice cream.

"Hi," Jenny said breathlessly. "You look like you swallowed a prune."

"What kept you so long?" I snapped, feeling annoyed.

She motioned to her cello, which was almost as large as she was.

"Oh," I said. "I'll carry your books." The disappointment inside about Robby was rising, but I kept it to myself. Jenny might have wanted to drive me crazy with another of her potions.

When we got to the brownstone, we carried Jenny's cello up the whole four flights. Exhausted, I went to pour us some ice-cold milk. That's when

Rabbit-sitting

I found a note: *Will be right back. Had to drop off the rush job. Feed Tabitha. The key is next to the stove. Love, Mom. P.S. Cookies from the bakery on the bottom shelf.*

"Should we wait until your mom gets back, or do we chance it alone?" Jenny fiddled with the magnets on the refrigerator, reading Mom's scribbling over my shoulder.

"We're together, right?" I said, grabbing the key.

We hastily made our way upstairs. Tabitha went crazy as we approached her hutch and I unlatched it. "She's starved," Jenny cooed, petting her.

"Only a handful of alfalfa pellets," I read to Jenny from a handwritten index card attached to the wire mesh. "And some rolled oats. Not too many, about a tablespoon."

While Jenny put food in the ceramic crock, I poured the old water down the drain. Then Jenny screamed.

"What?" I yelled, continuing to fill the water bottle under the faucet.

Jenny just pointed as she ran around the room in circles like a chicken in a coop. "Tabitha's gone!"

"What?" I ran over to the hutch.

"I mean, she jumped out!"

Then I saw Tabitha squirm around the crack between the door and the wall. "Why didn't you

THE FORTUNETELLER IN 5B

shut the door after I unlocked it?" I cried. "You came in after me."

"I felt safer with the door open a little."

"Great. Just what we needed."

We heard cries from downstairs. "Wild beast!"

Mrs. Pearlstein was chasing Tabitha with the end of a vacuum cleaner. I was afraid she'd suck in her tail.

"Get that wild rodent out of here!"

"Sorry!" I shouted over the rumbling noise, trying desperately to scoop up the rabbit in my arms. When I finally caught Tabitha, I held her firmly until she was safe in her hutch. She made these loud thumping sounds, vibrating the cage on the floor. "Could that be the infamous spirit of 5B?" I turned to Jenny.

"The haunting of Alexandria Pilaf." Jenny pretended she was floating around the apartment like a ghost.

We burst out laughing. "You little devil, you." I stared at Tabitha, innocently standing on her hind legs, begging like a dog. "Doesn't Mrs. Pearlstein know rabbits aren't rodents?" I scratched her behind the ears. "To think I lost any sleep because of you." And I touched her nose playfully. "We need to change the newspaper in this tray. I saw some over there." I pointed to a rocker outside the large walk-in closet.

Rabbit-sitting

"Allie!" Jenny shouted. She rippled her hand across the beaded curtain, creating an opening. The glass beads broke the light into tiny rainbows on the floor and ceiling.

"What now?" I groaned.

"Come here."

The glittering ropes clinked as I walked through. I remained still at first. If I crossed that threshold, what would I find? Would I want to know?

The door to the closet was wide open. Jenny and I looked at each other, and then at the small room. She started moving toward the inside. "Where are you going?" I tugged at her wrist.

"One quick peek won't hurt. It's just us. Who will know?"

"It doesn't feel right," I said, frightened. And yet I allowed Jenny to lead me farther into the closet, once again fascinated by the objects on the walls, the smells, this time like root beer or wintergreen and maybe, the presence of Madame Van Dam herself.

We stared at the rug that had covered the trunk. It was now rolled up and draped over Madame Van Dam's chair.

"Her crystal ball is gone," I said.

"I noticed that too," Jenny said, touching everything.

THE FORTUNETELLER IN 5B

A painted egg in a moldy bird's nest nearly rolled off a shelf onto the floor. My heart stopped. "Be careful!" I cried.

"I am," Jenny said indignantly, nestling it back in the rotting nest.

When she was done staring at the worn books lining one wall, she turned and yanked at the latch on the trunk. It appeared locked, but to our shock and surprise, the lock gave way, sounding a loud clump on the wooden floor. We both jumped.

"We shouldn't be here." I turned to go, and Jenny grabbed me.

"But we *are* here. And we've been dying to see what's inside ever since she moved in."

"These are Madame Van Dam's private things."

"You know as well as I do that we're not leaving until we see what's inside."

She carefully lifted the heavy top. On a first glimpse, it looked like a lot of junk and old clothes. Jenny slipped on some gold necklaces. "Take them off," I insisted as she bent down and gathered letters bunched together by a yellow silk ribbon. Rumanian stamps were glued on the top envelope. *Bucharest* was printed in magenta ink. Dad always got me stamps in mint condition from the post office.

"They're addressed to a Sophia Silver. In Queens," Jenny said.

Rabbit-sitting

"Put them back in the same spot you found them."

"I will," she snarled. "Stop worrying."

A dried rose corsage crumbled as Jenny tucked the letters back in the corner. She tried to piece in the petals, which turned to dust.

"Now look what you've done!" I shouted, and shook my head, feeling sick inside.

Jenny was clearly upset as she stooped to pick up the debris from the floor. Near the edge of the trunk also lay a photo. It must have slipped out of a letter.

"Which one?" I asked, scared.

"I don't know," Jenny whined, examining the photo more closely. "It's a picture of a girl our age in a Gypsy costume."

"And a younger girl too," I added.

"Do you think one of the children is Madame Van Dam with her parents? It's the same people in the photograph over Tabitha's hutch. Look, her father's holding a violin."

"But she said the one in her living room was the only picture she had of them." I felt confused.

Jenny turned the faded photo over. On the back was written: *Uncle Nicolae and Aunt Yvonne's Wedding, 1939.*

"She looks like a happy twelve-year-old there," I said.

THE FORTUNETELLER IN 5B

"Alexandria!" A muffled cry came through the front door.

"My mother!" I gasped, nearly closing the lid of the trunk on Jenny's fingers.

I took one last look at the room, trying to remember how everything was placed, praying it still remained as we found it. Then I ran to open the door.

"Didn't you hear me calling and knocking? What were you two doing?" My mother looked bothered.

"Nothing. Just cleaning up. Sorry, the water must have been running," I said, trying to sound casual. I couldn't bear to look at Jenny as she clumsily rushed through the beaded curtain, or at my mother.

CHAPTER TWELVE

Alias Madame Van Dam

There were so many unanswered questions. I wished Dad were here and I could tell him while he counted my freckles what I had discovered. Should I tell my mother? Or would she yell? I was afraid to return to 5B tomorrow after school. All those letters postmarked from Rumania to Sophia Silver. I drifted off to sleep.

Tuesday and Wednesday, I rushed in and out of the apartment as if it were on fire. I felt bad for Tabitha, who acted like she wanted some attention, but I was too frightened to stay—as though I were being watched. Jenny had to practice cello after school, so she conveniently didn't help me. The mysterious woman who had called Madame Van Dam "my silver jewel" showed up on Thursday

THE FORTUNETELLER IN 5B

while I was brushing Tabitha. I told her Madame Van Dam was away and would be back sometime over the weekend. Sophia Silver? My *silver* jewel?

On Saturday, Jenny called. "Do you want to go to the movies?"

"I have to do a final cleaning of the hutch before Madame Van Dam returns," I said coldly. We fell silent to secrets we shared about Madame Van Dam's past. Secrets we didn't understand.

"I could meet you at the matinee," Jenny said. "First show's at noon. I'd wait at the candy counter."

"If I'm not there, go in without me."

It was raining and muggy outside, and I guess everyone had the same idea. Robby Berkert was sitting with his friends three rows in front of us. As we waited for the movie to begin, Lindsay Blum strolled down the aisle holding a giant bucket of popcorn. She sat down next to them.

I sprang up from my seat and rushed toward the bathroom. Jenny followed. "What's wrong?" I could hear her voice behind me.

"Allie," Jenny begged over the door of the locked stall between us. "Come on out."

"Leave me alone." I sniffled, and blew my nose into some toilet paper. I felt like shouting, I can't trust you anymore.

"Robby Berkert is no big deal."

"Nothing's a big deal with you."

Alias Madame Van Dam

"What's that supposed to mean?"

"I spent an entire week alone in that apartment feeling like a criminal. You left me alone to pick up the pieces." And I threw up in the toilet bowl.

"Are you okay?" Jenny pounded on the door to the stall as she heard me gagging.

I coughed, wiping my lips. They felt parched. I unlocked the door. Jenny handed me a moist paper towel. I lifted my hair and blotted the back of my neck.

"Wash your face," she ordered, turning on the faucet. Then she put her arm around me. "You're my best friend; please don't be mad."

"What we did wasn't nice. Going into Madame Van Dam's trunk."

"You're right," Jenny admitted. "But weren't you curious too?"

I nodded. I had to be honest. In my heart, I had wanted to know what was inside that trunk.

As we heard the movie beginning outside, Jenny whispered, "Ignore Lindsay Blum. Pray she chokes on Jujyfruits and everyone gets sudden amnesia on how to do the Heimlich maneuver."

I dug my hands into the pockets of my jeans as we returned to the back row of the darkened theater. Jason Rosenthal and Craig Benson, two guys from our class, sat in front of us. We swapped half of their Raisinets and some popcorn for half

THE FORTUNETELLER IN 5B

of Jenny's giant-size box of Goobers during the rest of the film.

When I got home, my mother said, "Madame Van Dam's back. She wanted her key."

I felt in the side pocket of my jeans. It was there. My stomach made one of those little flips like I get before a major test or a big soccer match. "I'll just go upstairs a sec," I said, trying to sound nonchalant. But my head ached as I climbed the steps.

I paused before I knocked at the door, staring at the brass number and letter 5B. There were a pair of wet galoshes on the straw mat and her umbrella, still dripping, beside them. Before I raised my hand to knock, the door suddenly opened. Was Madame Van Dam really psychic? Would she instantly know what we had done? My hand trembled as I drew the key from my pocket and handed it to her.

"Thank you. Seems like Tabitha was well cared for. Come in. I have a little something for you." She put her frail fingers around my arm, guiding me into her apartment. All I could think was, How fast could I get out of here?

Madame Van Dam unfastened the buckles on her leather suitcase and placed a rounded bunch of tissue paper in my hands. "For me?" I said.

"You took care of someone very important to

me." She picked up Tabitha, settling the rabbit in her lap, and looked down, rubbing her like a cat. Tabitha didn't move.

I carefully unwrapped the layers of paper, unfolding them like leaves of lettuce. When I got to the center, there was a small crystal ball on a solid black base. It wasn't as large as Madame Van Dam's, but it was a perfectly round beautiful one.

"I bought it in Atlantic City. I was a fortune-teller at a convention down there. I said to myself, That nice girl downstairs might like this."

"This is for *me?*" I felt awful. Absolutely terrible. If she only knew what Jenny and I had done. "I can't accept it," I said.

"Why not? You don't like it?"

"It's wonderful."

"My mother gave me a large one at your age. That was the last thing she ever gave me. It's odd how unimportant objects can become important ones and have value far beyond their price tag."

I thought of the orange crate my father turned into a dollhouse. He sawed out little windows and doors, and made partitions for the bedrooms. There was a hole in the top floor for a staircase down to the first. I spent hours sewing tiny curtains and matching bedspreads for the miniature toothpick and Popsicle stick beds. Mom wanted to throw the dollhouse out when we moved because we had so

THE FORTUNETELLER IN 5B

little room, but I insisted on keeping it even though I hadn't played with it in years.

"Well," I said awkwardly, "my mom's waiting for me."

"Thank you, again."

"Thank you," I said, motioning to the crystal ball I had left on the kitchen table beside a stack of unopened mail addressed to a Sophia Silver. As I glanced down, my heart froze. Next to the pile of letters was a photograph. Was it the one that had slipped out from the letters in the trunk? Looking at it upside down, I wasn't sure. Why had she said that the photograph over the hutch was all she had? Was that the only one she could face? I knew I had a very hard time browsing through photographs of me and Dad from when I was little. Madame Van Dam saw me staring at it.

She pointed to the girl with braids wearing a peasant blouse and skirt. "Me at your age. At my uncle's wedding."

Yes, I know, I thought.

"Who's that next to you?"

"My sister." She swallowed.

"How old was she there?"

"Two years younger than me."

"Oh," I said. "My closest friend, Jenny, some-times feels like a sister." Lately, I didn't even know if I wanted her as a friend.

Alias Madame Van Dam

Madame Van Dam had that faraway look of hers. "A friend is a friend. Blood is blood."

Then she tucked the photo in the pocket of her apron.

"I found the photo on the floor of my closet. Strange," she said, her voice drifting off.

Was Madame Van Dam asking me to admit what I had done? Or was she not sure?

I was beginning to feel that for now what I learned about my neighbor was between us: me and Sophia Silver, alias, or otherwise known as, Madame Van Dam. And maybe for Jenny having Madame Van Dam as my neighbor was a game of witches and vampires, but for me knowing her was something more, whatever that more was.

CHAPTER THIRTEEN

Past Life

A week passed, and I realized I was trying to avoid Madame Van Dam. Until she told me for certain that she was Sophia Silver, she'd remain Madame Van Dam for me. I think she always would. One afternoon as I was coming home from school and walking up the steps to the fourth floor, she was coming down.

She came toward me, very deliberately, thrusting out her palm. "Is this yours?"

My red enamel barrette with the tiny hand-painted flowers was in the center of her hand. It was my favorite one. The one I had made at sleep-away camp. I thought it had been missing since the day Jenny and I had searched the trunk. Why didn't

Past Life

I risk looking for it? Because I couldn't bear to go back into that closet.

"Y-yes," I stammered, too afraid to ask where she had found it.

Her eyes looked hard. Not kind, like the time she gave me the crystal ball. She had trusted me. And I had let her down. I had let myself down. Without even yelling, she turned on her heel to leave.

"Madame Van Dam, Madame Van Dam!" I shouted after her. "I'm sorry. Please." But all I heard was the slam of the door to 5B.

That night Tabitha was thumping above me while I couldn't sleep. Was Tabitha afraid too? Of what? I tossed and turned and had bad dreams. At one point I woke suddenly, and sat up in bed. It was so strange. I felt as if my father were standing next to my night table, as though he were here beside me.

In the morning, the weather was overcast and gloomy as I waited for the school bus. I felt quiet inside. At lunch Jenny asked, "What's the matter?"

I just shrugged. "Nothing," I said.

Later at home while I was doing my homework, it began to drizzle. Slightly. The sound was peaceful as the rain pattered on the windowsill next to my desk. I pushed back my chair as I heard footsteps overhead. Edging my way outside into the hall, I listened, trying to peer over the banister at the fifth floor. There were loud clumping sounds. This time, without hesitating, I rushed upstairs, when now more than ever I should have waited because I was afraid of what might happen. The door to the roof was wide open. I climbed the ladder to the top. Madame Van Dam was standing near the edge picking dead leaves off the rows of geraniums and petunias Mrs. Pearlstein had planted in window boxes to line the fence surrounding the roof. City lights from other buildings glistened on the petals.

At first, I stayed back toward the door, watching. She swirled around, saw me, and turned away. I came closer. "I was wrong," I said.

"You had no business," she muttered.

"I know."

"Then why?"

"Ever since the day you moved in and the trunk was in the laundry room, and then it disappeared, my friend Jenny and I wondered where? How? And what was inside? We were curious."

I bit my lower lip and nervously fumbled with my hair clip, the one she had found.

"You wanted to know, so know!" She stared straight at me. "My sister, the one in the photo you misplaced in the bunch of letters from a friend, was murdered in a concentration camp—Zigeunerlager, which was the Gypsy camp near Birkenau, where they kept the Jews. Separate from us. Both were part of the Auschwitz complex of camps. My mother never understood why we were there. We were Christians. I never understood why anyone was there. My mother died of starvation and a broken heart without her little girl. She wanted to stay alive for my sake, and tried, but she just couldn't. My father played his violin in the camp orchestra. He 'welcomed' the prisoners as they came off trains from all over Europe. Later, he played for them as they walked toward the crematoriums, before they were gassed. In the end, the Nazis gassed him when he was too weak to play. I remained useful, though I could barely work. Other Gypsies took care of me the best they could." Madame Van Dam said this without any emotion, except when she stumbled over the word *useful*.

Could I live without *both* my parents? I listened, without asking, How did she? For the first time, even in the darkness, under the glow of the lights, I noticed a *Z* with four numbers tattooed on her arm. I knew that was her identification in the camp. I had seen it once before on someone on the bus and had asked my mother what it was, and she told me.

"At the end of the war, when the Americans freed us, a close friend of my mother's got me on

THE FORTUNETELLER IN 5B

a boat to the United States, where I lived in New York with a distant cousin. You had to have proof of a place to live. Often a relative. But many orphans were on that boat. Like me. I stayed with people during the trip who were blacksmiths, silversmiths, coppersmiths, some who had made pots. We were poor and traveled steerage. Refugees with money entered this country through New Jersey. At the end of the voyage when we came off the boat at Ellis Island, the guard asked the people I was with what they did for a living. Not knowing any English, the guard interpreted for us, and gave us all the last names of Smith or Silver. Not Gypsy names. My first name was Sophia after a friend who had helped my mother give birth to me, and then helped me once again find a new beginning. She's still in Rumania. She saved the dress and the photo I have now. I kept the other photo of my parents and sister hidden in a slat where I slept in the camp. Anyway, that's how I got the name Sophia Silver."

I thought of the hundreds of photographs of me and my family, tucked away in cartons, barely noticed. Once a year, we might take out an album or two during Thanksgiving, when all the relatives sat around full after dinner, with nothing to do but talk about the past and how young they all looked.

I wanted to ask how she got the name Madame Van Dam, but I waited as she continued. "The stench on that boat. Sweat. Vomit. Excrement. The camp was even worse. And the cattle car to the camp. No air. A tiny slit at the top. I was too short to feel any breeze between all the human bodies that held each other up. The first thing I did when we came down the ramp from the train was to lift my face into the rain." She raised her face toward the sky, closing her eyes. "All I smelled was an awful burning smell. Who knew it was flesh? How could I have known? I was a child. Tonight . . ." She took in a deep breath, and let it out. "Tonight feels clean and good." Drizzle misted my face.

I thought of the first time it rained after we buried my father. I cried myself to sleep because I hated the idea of him alone cold and outside. I wanted Mom to drive to the cemetery and put a blanket over his grave. To keep him warm and dry. It was crazy. I felt the same way during the first snow. I guess there was a first for everything.

Her face seemed to ease a little. That was when I asked, "How did you get the name Madame Van Dam, then?"

"Oh, later on, this cousin and I moved to the basement apartment of a narrow house overlooking the Long Island Expressway. The whole area is industrial now except for a few houses which remain near a sign that says 'Last Exit Before Toll.' The name of the street happens to be Van Dam. I moved

THE FORTUNETELLER IN 5B

and lived for many years in a Rumanian community in Queens not too far away. But when the elevated train was built nearby, people stopped coming off the street one flight up to let me read their palms or tea leaves. And it was just too noisy for my customers when I told their fortunes. My tailoring business also wasn't the same. The neighborhood had changed. I needed a change. I was doing a series of programs at the Y on how to read tarot cards and saw an ad for this apartment in a newsletter that goes out to all the Y's. So I answered, figuring this was a family building. I needed that."

"And the trunk, how did you get that upstairs?"

She paused, seeming to be trying to remember. "A customer of mine, a dancer in a club who I make costumes for, has four brothers in the circus. They came early one morning and dragged it up for me."

The drizzle turned into a heavy downpour. Madame Van Dam bolted the door to the roof as I climbed down the ladder and brushed myself off. "Like the first night we met," she said. She smiled slightly, but smiled.

"I'll never forget it," I replied. Then I felt uncomfortable as we stood in the hall in front of her apartment. Uncomfortable about all that I knew. That I had been waiting to know. And now that I knew, what could I say? "My life seems like nothing compared to yours," I said apologetically.

Past Life

She looked at me, her forehead wrinkling. "Don't ever say that. A life is a life. You don't have to measure if your loss is less or more than mine. You shouldn't feel guilty. A bucket full of water can be full. So can a thimble. Full is full. Empty is empty." But in my heart I felt that her loss was greater.

"Just a minute," Madame Van Dam said to me, going into 5B and then coming out into the hall. "You forgot this. Please. I want you to have it." And she handed me the small crystal ball.

"Thank you," I said hesitantly.

"Enjoy it," she said, "as I have enjoyed mine."

When I got downstairs into my room, I unwrapped the crystal ball and sat cross-legged on the bed in the dark, listening to the rain. I shut my eyes. All I could see was Madame Van Dam on the roof with her eyes closed, lifting her face into the rain. Then in my mind I saw the photo of Sophia Silver. Little Sophie, who at my age had no one. Absolutely no one. I shook inside. She was alone. She survived both parents dying. And her sister. And their dying horrible, unimaginable deaths. Worse than Dad's cancer? Then I thought of how she said not to measure. How could you measure feelings? They were what they were. Down deep, though, I couldn't help feeling that compared to her, I had no right to long after a year and a half

THE FORTUNETELLER IN 5B

for us to be a family again: me, Mom, and Dad. But wasn't it around fifty years later for her, and wasn't she in a way still mourning too?

I felt dumb that I had been depressed about finding Robby Berkert eating popcorn with Lindsay Blum. Look what was happening to Madame Van Dam at my age. How could I even comprehend it? Then I realized she wasn't expecting me to.

CHAPTER FOURTEEN

Exit 49 South

I had all this feeling inside me that I didn't know what to do with. The light filtered under the crack of my bedroom door. It was probably coming from Mom's lamp attached to her drawing table. I opened the door and approached my mother. She was stooped over, working, and glanced up when I stood next to her. She paused, her brush midair, and I hugged her, extra tight. My lower lip quivered.

"What?" Mom asked, concerned. "What's the matter?"

That was when I began to cry. Without stopping. At first I couldn't even talk. Mom held me. Silently we remained, surrounded by the darkness of this one room. "Ma," I said.

THE FORTUNETELLER IN 5B

"Get it out," Mom said gently. "What is it?" she coaxed.

I told her everything. Everything there was to tell about Madame Van Dam. What Jenny and I had done, invading her privacy. That night on the roof when Sophia Silver told me about her family.

Once again, Mom pressed her lips to my forehead. I felt sick in a different way than the time I got my period. The feeling went even deeper inside. Toward an emptiness.

"Do you still love me?"

She moved me back by my shoulders. "I told you I'll always love you. Love has nothing to do with this. You know you were wrong. Madame Van Dam has had a very hard life, and you didn't make it any easier."

I gulped at those words. "I really am sorry. I'm not perfect."

"No one is. Everyone has done bad things in their lives. You have to own up to it, handle it the right way. Did you?"

"I tried."

"Then that's all anyone can ask. We must learn from our mistakes and go on."

My mother led me back to bed, tucking me in. She sat on the edge for several extra minutes. "So why don't I feel better?" I asked.

"Everything takes time. There are no quick

remedies. For anything. You learn that as you get older." She pushed the covers over my shoulders and kissed me good night.

"Leave the light on in the bathroom," I said as she was leaving.

Mom turned around and smiled. Then she walked over and switched on the light, the same way she did when I was little and scared.

I watched across the hall as she bent over the bathroom sink, squirting drops in her eyes. It reminded me of the time Mom had a bad eye infection and Dad put the drops in for her. He had to lead her by the elbow across the street because her vision was blurry—just like he led me on my first day of kindergarten, holding my hand tightly before the crossing guard said we could go. I remembered looking at them not as my parents crossing Madison Avenue, but as two separate people from me, people who clearly cared so much for each other. That was the day we found out Dad had six months to live. His cancer was incurable. The tumor was in a spot the doctor just couldn't get to. "Inoperable," he had said. And I wondered, Who would put Mom's drops in her eyes?

The following morning Mom said, "I rented a car. We're going to see your father." I got this funny look on my face because I wasn't quite sure how I felt about that. "It will be okay," she said. "We'll be there together." She squeezed my shoulder. "Don't worry." Was she assuring herself or me?

We drove out along the Long Island Expressway to Exit 49 South. The trip felt like forever. Mom listened to an old tape of the Rolling Stones. The one she used to dance to with Dad. We passed graves lined in neat rows with endless fields of crosses. When that ended, acres away were graves that had Hebrew on the headstones. And the names changed from O'Reilly to Shapiro. Even in death, people seemed to need to be separated. When we got to the cemetery, Mom didn't know where to go, so she turned into a road that led to the main office. She went in alone as I sat in the car. She came out holding two small index cards. At the top they said, *Kaddish: Prayer for the Dead*. She handed me one. It was in Hebrew.

We parked the car close to the grave site. I locked my arm in Mom's as we walked through several rows. There were hardly any trees. Off in the distance was a large bulldozer. When we finally found where Dad was, it didn't seem real seeing his name on the tombstone. Mom squatted down and began tugging at some weeds, pulling them away from a small clump of purple wildflowers. "What kind are these?" I asked, but my mother didn't seem to hear me.

Exit 49 South

"He never liked crabgrass," she said without looking up as she pulled at some more, trying to make the grass look neat and trim beneath the name Ian Pilaf, beloved husband, father, and son.

I stooped down and joined my mother.

"In the fall, I'm going to plant cheerful red tulips. Bright, happy, large scarlet ones that will grow high in the spring."

"I'll help you, Ma, if you want."

"Only if you want," she said. "It would have been twenty-one years this winter."

"That's a long time being married," I said.

Mom sighed. Her cheeks were wet, streaming with tears as she recited Kaddish. "I miss that man so much," Mom said. "He was my best friend."

I missed Dad for Mom. I missed Dad for me.

She placed a small pebble on Dad's headstone. We did that for Dad's father once. To show we'd been there. That someone had come, and remembered the dead. I picked up a tiny grayish blue stone, which reminded me of the color of his eyes, and placed it next to my mother's. Then I found three more. One for each of Madame Van Dam's parents. One for her nine-year-old sister. For the graves they never had.

Before we wandered back to the car, Mom turned to have one last look. Her knees wobbled. We found a bench on a slight hill under a tree and

THE FORTUNETELLER IN 5B

sat down. I was glad we were alone and nobody else was nearby. I would have hated that.

"Do you believe in life after death?" I asked.

"Oh, hon, I don't know about anything anymore."

"Yes, you do," I said softly.

"I'd like to think that it goes on—that there's more."

"Then you could see Dad again."

She smiled. "My Alex, my Big Al," she imitated Dad as she stroked my hair. "Make the most of what's here. Life is short sometimes. There are so many wonderful things, too. Love. Children. Work."

"And pizza," I said.

"And egg rolls," Mom added. She put her arms around me and kissed the top of my head, breathing in deeply. "We're surviving, Alex, without him. We'll be okay. We *are* okay, aren't we?"

I smiled, hoping. I could almost feel my father next to us on the bench, listening, me being the salami between their two slices of rye bread. But Mom said now we'd have to go on, open faced.

"I can't lie," Mom continued. "It will never be the same again. There will always be something missing, but think of all he added to our lives. That can never be taken away. All those memories."

I thought of Sophia Silver and all the memories

she had to live with. I figured if she could survive after what she had seen and been through, and could even laugh, then I could too. That things in life would be okay like Mom said, and that people could feel joy even after great pain if they tried very hard and worked to capture happiness, which is what Madame Van Dam must have meant in her tent at the street fair when she read my fortune. My father wasn't in a small plot of land, he was in my heart. Forever.

CHAPTER FIFTEEN

If I Only Had a Crystal Ball

Grandma always said to Mom, "If I only had a crystal ball, we'd all be rich." What Grandma didn't realize was that we were. Not in the way of money. In other ways. The ways that count. Grandma had Grandpa. Mom and I had each other. And that was a lot more than Madame Van Dam ever had, or ever would have. I still couldn't get used to thinking of her as Sophia Silver. To me, she'd always be the fortuneteller in 5B. The woman with the gray frizzy hair and black rabbit who moved in during a terrible thunderstorm a year and a half after my father died. I had to tell Jenny who she really was. Now that I was one hundred percent sure. Jenny's parents invited me to go out to dinner with them on Saturday night. Fancy-shmancy. I decided to break the news

If I Only Had a Crystal Ball

as we waited for a table in the lounge. Jenny's parents were talking to two actors as we watched tropical fish in a saltwater tank.

"Jenny," I said, fussing with the bow in my hair as she followed the route with her finger of a swift cobalt blue fish dodging around an orange plastic plant. I tapped the tank to get her attention.

"Look at the colors on that striped fish under the toy diver!"

"Jenny," I repeated, "Madame Van Dam is Sophia Silver."

"I figured that after we found the bundle of letters from Rumania in the trunk," she said, seeming to be more interested in the fuchsia gravel than my news.

Jenny was so casual after all that time spent wondering, pretending, kidding ourselves that Madame Van Dam was something other than she was. Maybe Jenny and I had thought about her in different ways because in the end it needed to be my discovery, not Jen's. Madame Van Dam and I were linked by loss, not by being neighbors, something Jenny couldn't completely understand and didn't have to, really.

"So now you know for sure that she's not a vampire or a witch," I teased.

"How does one ever know *that* for sure?" she said, raising her eyebrows.

THE FORTUNETELLER IN 5B

"She told me who she really is." I cleared my throat. "Her entire family was murdered in a concentration camp during World War II. Her parents. Her younger sister. Every one of them. Dead."

Jenny stared at a fish trapped in a corner by a larger one.

"She was an orphan at our age?" Jenny looked over at me and slumped her shoulders. Her braid reminded me of the photo of Madame Van Dam at her uncle's wedding where she looked so happy. "We're lucky, aren't we?"

I nodded, thinking I'd tell Jenny the details about how they died only if she asked. And not here. Later. After I was ready to absorb them myself. If I'd ever be ready.

"She gave me a present for taking care of Tabitha. A crystal ball," I said.

"A crystal ball!" Jenny shouted. Some people nearby turned around. She lowered her voice. "To see into the future. This is great, Allie." And she got a far-off, mysterious look.

"I thought you don't believe in all that stuff now," I teased again.

"Well," Jenny said confidently, "you just never know when a crystal ball will come in handy."

"Here we go again." I smiled. The maitre d' called the name Bolero, and Jenny's parents said good-bye to the actors.

If I Only Had a Crystal Ball

We were guided toward the prettiest table, in the center of the room under a huge skylight. Hanging ferns with moss flowing from the pots and cheerful pink geraniums trailed the ceiling. A waiter pulled my chair out and seated me next to a pine tree dotted with tiny white lights glowing, in June!

"Feels like Christmas!" Jenny beamed.

It really did feel like a holiday.

After dinner, Mr. and Mrs. Bolero waited until I got safely into the brownstone. Mom was sitting up in bed with letters strewn all over the entire quilt.

"What are you doing?" I asked, sitting next to her.

She paused from her reading. "What, sweetheart? Had a nice time?"

"Those." I pointed to the letters and some photos.

"Oh, these." She shuffled the few in her lap. The light from the lamp glowed on Dad's tight, neat handwriting. "They're from your father. Letters he wrote to me during the Vietnam War. I thought it was about time I reread them. Took them out. Something I've been avoiding."

"Dad's?" I edged closer.

"Letters home from before you were ever even thought of."

"Not even a little zygote?" I teased, showing

off what we had just learned in our health and science unit.

"Not even a single cell." She handed me a leaf of crisp paper. "It's okay. You can read it. I want you to."

It started off, *Dear Dune*.

"Who's Dune?" I asked.

"Oh." She giggled like Jenny and I did when we saw cute boys. "Your silly father used to call me that after the cookie, Lorna Doone. He said that I was much sweeter." Mom rolled her eyes, and I rolled mine. I continued to read:

Hi, Babes. How's life in the States? My hair looks like one of those cheap nylon brushes. I miss your fingers running through my long blond locks (sappy, huh?), but my sergeant said, "Pilaf, you look like some sissy in a beauty parlor. Or one of those peace-loving hippies." And he said a few other things that I won't repeat. The guy who bunks next to me also comes from New York. Kew Gardens, actually. He also had a low draft number in the lottery. When I told him mine was 27, he couldn't believe it. I still can't. The weather stinks. It rains a lot. The flies are driving me nuts. I feel like I live in mud. What I wouldn't do for a steaming hot bath. Why torture myself? Remember that tub with the club feet standing in the middle of the bathroom when we went to Block Island for our honeymoon? And that old man walked in on

If I Only Had a Crystal Ball

us brushing our teeth. Sorry I couldn't afford a better place. You still seemed to like it. Oh, babes. When I come home, a suite at the Plaza, right? Still, riding the tandem around the island was the best. And finding those fresh green peas growing near the ocean, shucking the pods, eating them raw for dinner. Geez, I can almost taste their sweetness. Keep my bicycle in shape. Okay? I'll need it when I get back. And maybe someday, instead of a bicycle built for two, we'll have one for three? Sound good? Hope I can come back to make it possible. Be good. Gotta go now. I'll write tomorrow. God, do I miss you. I love you. Always will.

Forever,
Ian

As I placed the letter back in my mother's hands, she tucked her chin over my head and stroked my hair. "Promise me you'll never throw these letters away."

"I promise," I said.

"Good." Mom sighed.

"Ma." She looked at me. "I was thought of. Dad wanted a bicycle built for three."

We drifted off to sleep in the peaceful quiet of the dimly lit room and awakened Sunday morning with the letters still scattered around us.

"Good morning," Mom said.

"Hi." I waved from under the covers and looked at her through tired, bleary eyes.

THE FORTUNETELLER IN 5B

"Today's a perfect day to go somewhere open and sunny."

"Where?" I yawned.

"You'll see. Get dressed."

Blueberry pancakes, Dad's favorite, were ready after I put on some fresh clothes. We gobbled them down, and Mom rushed me out of the apartment. Madame Van Dam was leaning on the ledge of her window next to a window box filled with more of her herbs as I waited for Mom to lock the outside door. She waved to me and held Tabitha next to her, waving Tabitha's silver-and-black paw in the air. I almost thought I saw Tabitha smile, but rabbits couldn't smile.

"*La revedere!* Good-bye!" she shouted down.

"Good-bye, Madame Van Dam!" I waved back up to her.

When I turned around at the end of the block to see if she was still there, she was gone. Completely. As if she had been a part of my imagination and not real.

"Stay close to me," my mother said.

I followed her across the street, down into the subway past the same man selling flowers who had given Madame Van Dam the bouquet of daisies on Mother's Day. We ended up on a train going out to Brooklyn.

If I Only Had a Crystal Ball

"Ma!" I yelled over the beat of a teenager's loud radio. "Where are we going?"

"You'll see."

As we got closer, I realized where my mother was leading me: on a trip I had often made with my father. Coney Island. Somehow, I didn't ever remember her in the picture of those memories.

It was the kind of day where the sun was glaring on the hot white sand. Dad would have loved taking me to see the beluga whales at the aquarium. We would have strolled on the boardwalk alongside the beach, and he would have told me about the Cyclone roller coaster that he went on as a kid, and how he threw up on his cousin Bruce afterward. As Mom and I walked by the old empty wooden Cyclone, Dad's roller coaster, past the steel Double Loop, a traveling one filled with riders, I missed him so much I ached inside. We passed by a sideshow with a tattooed lady, a snake charmer, and a woman with a flaming red turban who could see into the future for one dollar, and the past for two. Maybe Madame Van Dam could let my father slip through from the other side for just one day? Today. But then if that really happened, I wouldn't want to let him go back. I'd want him to see me on my first date, graduating from college, and maybe having my own children someday—all the things

THE FORTUNETELLER IN 5B

he'd miss. That I'd have without him. I even wanted him to see that I was doing okay. That Mom was okay, too. That we'd never get over him like people say you should after a while, because the feeling of missing doesn't go away like a bad cold. The pain changes. That's all. I guess if you were here, Dad, I'd say that I just wasn't ready to have you leave so soon. You didn't even get a chance to see me try to score the winning goal for this season's soccer games and "blossom into a young lady," like Mom says I have. But then, who knows—according to our neighbor in 5B, maybe you did?

AUTHOR'S NOTE

Terezin was a concentration camp where Jews were held until they were sent to Auschwitz to be exterminated. Fifteen thousand children passed through the camp of Terezin from 1941 to 1945. One hundred survived. One who did not was Frantisek Bass, born in 1930, deported to Terezin in 1942. Almost the same age as Allie. The same age as Madame Van Dam when she was in a concentration camp. Not quite twelve years old. This boy was murdered at Auschwitz in 1944. He left a poem. It is part of the Musaf Service in the prayer book at my synagogue during Yom Kippur, which is the holiest Jewish holiday, where we make peace and ask forgiveness for the wrongs we have done during the past year. This is a small part of his poem:

A little garden,
Fragrant and full of roses.
The path is narrow,
And a little boy walks along it.

A little boy, a sweet boy,
Like that growing blossom.
When the blossom comes to bloom,
The little boy will be no more.

Six million little boys and girls,
    and men and women,
Six million of our cousins
Who by the whim of monsters are no more.

That little boy, my cousin,
Whose cry might have been my cry
    in that dark land—
Where shall I seek you?
There's not anywhere a tomb, a mound, a sod,
    a broken stick
Marking the sepulchres.

ABOUT THE AUTHOR

JANE BRESKIN ZALBEN is the author of a number of middle-grade and young adult novels, as well as her series of Jewish holiday picturebooks. She is currently teaching illustration, design, and writing picturebooks at the School of Visual Arts.

Ms. Zalben lives in Sands Point, New York, with her husband and two sons.

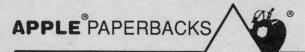

APPLE® PARERBACKS

Pick an Apple and Polish Off Some Great Reading!

BEST-SELLING APPLE TITLES

❏ MT43944-8	**Afternoon of the Elves** Janet Taylor Lisle	$2.75
❏ MT43109-9	**Boys Are Yucko** Anna Grossnickle Hines	$2.95
❏ MT43473-X	**The Broccoli Tapes** Jan Slepian	$2.95
❏ MT42709-1	**Christina's Ghost** Betty Ren Wright	$2.75
❏ MT43461-6	**The Dollhouse Murders** Betty Ren Wright	$2.75
❏ MT43444-6	**Ghosts Beneath Our Feet** Betty Ren Wright	$2.75
❏ MT44351-8	**Help! I'm a Prisoner in the Library** Eth Clifford	$2.95
❏ MT44567-7	**Leah's Song** Eth Clifford	$2.75
❏ MT43618-X	**Me and Katie (The Pest)** Ann M. Martin	$2.95
❏ MT41529-8	**My Sister, The Creep** Candice F. Ransom	$2.75
❏ MT46075-7	**Sixth Grade Secrets** Louis Sachar	$2.95
❏ MT42882-9	**Sixth Grade Sleepover** Eve Bunting	$2.95
❏ MT41732-0	**Too Many Murphys** Colleen O'Shaughnessy McKenna	$2.75